Each year, approximately 16,000 people are murdered in the United States. Seven percent of the killers are female; one of them being Simone Campbell. In *Secrets of a Side Bitch 2*, Simone is struggling to keep together the web of lies that she has woven, all in attempts to be the number one woman in Omari Sutton's life. She continues to pull one devious and demented trick after another to maintain her role as Omari's leading lady. Her tower of lies begins crashing down as intricate parts of her schemes begin to unfold. Chance reemerges, threatening Simone's connection to the murder. Desperateness to have Omari's baby sends Simone into such erratic behavior that she starts to make telling mistakes.

All the while, Omari is set on making Aeysha's murderer pay for killing the one woman that truly had his heart.

FEMISTRY PRESS PUBLICATIONS
A self-publishing entity
info@femistrypress.net
wholesale@femistrypress.net
www.jessica-n-watkins.com

Femistry Press Paperback Printing
Smart Black Rich Publications Digital Printing

Cover Art by TSPub Creative

Three months ago…

Omari

I laughed at the way Capone smiled at me when I walked into the bar.

"Get that goofy ass grin off your face, nigga. You done got soft in two months?"

We shook up, but considering what I had been through, Capone gave me a bro hug.

"Man, I can't front. It's good to see you out and about."

It felt good being out and about. The last two months after Aeysha's murder had been rough, to say the least. For weeks after the funeral, I stayed in the house, trying hard to stay sane. I didn't eat much. I could never sleep. I even got fired from UPS because I was taking too much time off.

Capone ordered me a shot of Patron. At first, I was scared to even drink that shit, thinking that my drunk mind would bring my grieving truth to the surface. Yea, I was outside, but it was all a front. I was pretending to have it all together for the sake of trying to press on.

Life was forcing me to keep living.

"I was surprised you called me, man."

I knew Capone would be surprised. But like I said, life was forcing me to keep living. "I know."

"What's up?"

"That offer still on the table to take over them blocks?"

Capone's eyes brightened with happiness. "You ready to work?"

I was more than ready. I couldn't stomach living in that apartment after Aeysha was killed. Because she was just as excited about the house in Riverdale as I was, I went ahead and moved in it, even though I was laid off. My stash had dwindled down to barely anything. I was still fucked up in the head about Aeysha, and I even still had a bad taste in my mouth about being in the game, since it's what led to her getting killed. But I was back at square one. I was back struggling to pay bills. And even though I didn't have Aeysha to take care of anymore, in addition to my mother, I still had a little Aeysha to take care of.

Dahlia Rose had survived the shooting. Though born at fourteen ounces and only ten inches long, after two months of being in the Neonatal Unit at Wyler's Children's Hospital, my little princess was being released from the hospital the next day.

"I'm more than ready," I told Capone.

"You got the bread?"

I didn't, but I knew who did.

Just as I nodded my head, Simone came into the bar. She looked good in a fitted leather blazer, knee length leather boots and straight leg jeans. Her hair bounced like she had just gotten it done. It was much longer and looked like that good virgin shit that women spend hundreds on. Even her body looked different. She was a lot more toned, and she had a lot more hips and ass than I remembered. I knew she'd gotten some money from selling her crib. I figured some of it had been injected in her ass.

Just like Capone, I had to laugh at the way she smiled at me.

"Heeeey," she sung to me as she hugged me. "It's good to see you."

I hadn't seen her since Aeysha was killed. We'd stayed in contact because she refused to let me slip past the point of no return. Day in and day out, Simone was talking to me, consoling me and helping me cope with the pain. Even though I was grieving, I couldn't deny how she had put her feelings aside just to be there for me while I grieved for my woman.

Because of that, my love for her had grown even more.

Even while I was trying to figure out how to get back on my feet, she offered to loan me the money that I needed to cop some weight from the connect.

She was willing to loan me twenty thousand dollars. She was loyal as fuck, and I appreciated it like a motherfucka.

"Look at you. You've lost so much weight."

Timidly, I smiled. When usually that was a good thing, for me, it was bad. I wasn't the biggest nigga before. After weeks of barely having an appetite, I'd lost muscle mass along with about twenty pounds.

"I know. I'm getting it back right, though. One day at a time."

"That's the only way to do it."

After ordering a drink, Simone got to the point. "So what's up? Why did you ask me to come here?"

Along with having Capone meet me so that I could get my shit rolling into the direction of getting my life back on track, I asked Simone to come for the same reasons.

"I needed to talk to you."

"About?"

"Well, besides my mother, you've been there for me through what is probably the worst thing I will ever go through in my life." Just thinking about it brought tears to my eyes. But I shook that feeling. Even if it was just a front, I had to move on. "I can't image how it must feel having feelings for somebody who loves somebody else. The fact that you put your feelings to the side just to be there for me is something that I will never forget. I've always liked you. And in a fucked up way, now I can be there for you like you have been there for me. I got this little girl coming home with me tomorrow. I don't know the first thing about raising a girl. It's so many things changing in my life, but I know for a fact that I want you in it helping me through the change."

Simone

As he said those words, my body literally exhaled.

"Of course, I'll be there for you."

Then, Omari reached out and hugged me. To be in his arms again was like taking a breath that I had been waiting to take for two months. I exhaled and engrossed myself in his arms.

As we let go, he gave me the most sensual kiss on the lips.

My arms were around his neck as I smiled flirtatious and said, "I missed you."

"I missed you too." When he spoke, those beautiful gray eyes were damn near sparkling.

Then, regret filled my heart as I felt my phone vibrating in my pocket. I knew it was Chance, so I had to go.

"Listen. I have to make a run. How long will you be here?"

"For awhile. Come back."

I promised Omari that I would as I finished off my drink. Then I hurried towards the door. Once outside, I literally ran to my car and away from the biting air. It was a cold December day- only thirty degrees.

No matter how cold it was outside, I was hot as hell on the inside with thoughts of Omari running through my mind as I turned on the radio.

"Yet another pregnant woman was gunned down on the Southside last night. Tina Presley, twenty-seven and four months pregnant was gunned down during a drive by on Seventy-Ninth and Racine. This is the second time this year a pregnant woman has been murdered by gun violence. Aeysha Richardson was gunned down just two months ago outside of her home. This violence has to…"

I shut the DJ up by turning off the radio.

Fuck that bitch! I was tired of hearing about Aeysha! She was dead, but I was hearing her fucking name more than I did when she was alive.

Urgh!

But all is well that ends *perfectly*. Finally, I had my man. No longer was I the bitch that lost to some other trick. Finally, after all of the planning, plotting, and scheming, I was number one and it felt so fucking good.

As I pulled into the gas station on Eighty-Seventh and State with the biggest smile on my face thinking of Omari, I spotted Chance standing in a black North Face bubble coat. I blew the horn. He spotted me and quickly came over to the car.

I popped the lock and reached for my purse. By the time he climbed in and shut the door, I handed him the blank envelope full of cash.

All he could say was, "Bet."

During this entire time, Chance had been very nonchalant about this whole thing. But he needed the money more than life itself, so I knew that, no matter his attitude, he would follow through with the plan.

"You're leaving town, right?"

He didn't have a choice really. Staying in Chicago was too risky. Even though Omari said that Aeysha's murder case had grown cold, I did not want to risk Chance lingering around Chicago.

As he opened the envelope and thumbed through the cash, he nodded slowly.

"It's all there," I assured him. "Twenty-five thousand dollars."

Twenty-five thousand dollars to kill that bitch Aeysha. I could not believe it. But, I can't even deny that when Omari wrapped his arms around me and kissed me, I felt like it was worth every penny. Besides, after killing Tammy, I was even more willing to pay someone to get rid of Aeysha for me.

Tammy had it coming though! I saw that bitch fucking Omari. The day I found out about Aeysha, I went to his house. I wasn't expecting to see anything. I just sat out there staring, wishing that I was the one living in there with him. When I saw him leave the house, I trailed him to that club. Then I just sat out there all night, wondering if I should go in. So I was parked a few cars down when him and Tammy got into the backseat of his car. A few days after that bitch had the nerve to look like she questioned if Omari was really my man, I went back over her mother's house to confront her "perfect" ass about fucking Omari.

You know what that bitch had the nerve to tell me? She had the audacity to call me crazy for following him. She called me a psycho stalker. Then she had the nerve to tell me that Omari wasn't my man and would never want me. She said that I would never be anything in my life but a side bitch.

I showed that bitch how he would never want her slut ass again when I choked her motherfuckin' ass to death.

I was just so mad that she was talking to me like that! She was right. After falling for another man, I was still playing second string to some bitch. I felt so stupid and so angry. And when Tammy sat there looking at me like I was worthless, I felt like Tammy had transformed into the main bitch to all them niggas that didn't choose me. So I leaped over and just started choking the bitch! I was choking her so hard that I could feel the ridges of her esophagus against my fingertips.

I was in a trance of rage. I honestly didn't realize what I was doing until she was taking her last breath. For thirty minutes, I sat there in shock wondering what the fuck to do with her body before her mother came home. Then I drug her body out to the garage and into my car, drove it to the forest preserve, and set her on fire to burn any evidence. I knew everybody would think it was Jimmy.

I felt bad, but I had always envied Tammy so much that I wished she would go away. Even when Jimmy would call me trying to find her, I would give him her new number and even told him where she was.

After getting away with killing Tammy, I was even more convinced to kill Aeysha, especially if I didn't do it myself. I had always planned to pay Chance to do the dirty work. At first, I put my mother's house up for sale to get the money to loan to Omari so that he could buy into Ching's camp. I figured that would be a way to get his attention again. But, as he distanced himself more and more, I figured I could use the money to pay Chance to get rid of Aeysha all together. Chance needed the money, he was a naive kid down on his luck that had a crush on me, and I needed him.

Since Aeysha was on bed rest, my plan that day was for Chance to break into the apartment and kill Aeysha. As Chance and I sat in my car at the end of the block, waiting on Omari to leave, never once did I think to stop, and neither did he. We both needed it for very different desperate reasons.

When we spotted her walking down the front steps, it was perfect timing.

I always had a gut feeling that once Aeysha was out of the picture, Omari would be all mine. Now, she had been completely erased from the gawd damn picture and finally, *finally,* I was number one.

Finally, I won.

Secrets of a Side Bitch 2

By Jessica N. Watkins

ONE

CHANCE

"What the fuck?"

I was so thrown off that my words left my lips in a whisper. My mouth hit the floor as I continued to look under the floorboard, wishing that the cocaine would appear in front of my eyes out of thin air. I even reached my hands inside, to feel around the corners of the hiding place that I'd created for the bricks, but there was nothing.

"*Shit*!"

I was freaking out. The two bricks that I copped the day before were gone. Except for a thousand dollars, that was last of the twenty-five thousand dollars that Simone had given me.

Without them bricks, I was ass out.

"Marlin! Yo', Marlin!"

I was yelling for my roommate, as I stood from the floor in the closet of my bedroom and ran out. I knew that he was somewhere in the basement apartment that we'd been sharing for the last month.

I didn't even really know this nigga. After killing Aeysha, I left Chicago like Simone told me to. I ended up in Minnesota, where most niggas went when they wanted to come up. For weeks, I stayed at a Best Western motel until I got cool with this nigga, Marlin, who I often ran into at a bar across the street from the motel. Once he found out that I was living in the motel, he offered me a place to sleep until I got a crib.

But I couldn't get a crib until I had some steady income. I was sitting on twenty-five g's that had been slowly dwindling by the day. I had to flip my bread and flip it quick. At that same bar, I had become cool with a few local niggas who I knew were serving. Last week, one of them supplied me with two kilos of cocaine that I planned to flip into at least sixty thousand dollars.

Besides the dude that I bought them from, Marlin was the only other person that knew that I had the drugs.

When I saw Marlin in his bedroom playing X-Box, I lost my fucking mind.

"Marlin, what the fuck happened to my shit, man?!"

I stepped on and over everything in my path; knocking over cups, end tables, and whatever else was in my way.

I was seeing red. Those kilos were the only thing

left to my name. Without them, I was broke, homeless, and with nothing.

I was so pissed that I grabbed Marlin by the collar and shook him like a ragdoll without even thinking. I was so pissed that I didn't even pay attention to the dude that was in the room playing Madden with him, until he was standing behind me putting a gun to my head.

"Hands off of him, nigga."

Instantly, I raised my hands in surrender. Immediately, I bitched up in order to save my life and get my bricks back.

"I just want to know where my shit is."

With a conniving smile, Marlin asked, "What shit?"

And just that quick, I forgot about the gun that was being pointed at my head.

I charged towards Marlin, shouting to the point that I was slobbering as the words rushed out of my throat. "My fucking drugs! Where are they…"

Whack!

Buddy standing behind me had ended my rage by slamming the butt of his pistol against my jaw.

Instantly, I felt the side of my face swell as I fought the urge to pass out. It was all that I could do to continue to stand on my own two feet.

3

"Man, Marlin, let me shoot this clown!"

Now the gun was pointing directly at my head as this motherfucka mean mugged the fuck outta me while biting down hard on his lip.

Marlin laughed. "Calm down. He ain't on shit. Are you, Chance?"

I couldn't even talk. The pain in my face was crazy. Besides, there were two of them, plus a gun, against me; a no name nigga in their hood with no money and nobody to have my back.

"Consider them bricks gone and yourself homeless. Get the fuck out of my crib. And quickly, before this trigger happy nigga kills you."

There wasn't shit that I could do but get shot if I wanted to put up a fight. Defeat filled my heart like a punk ass fifth grader. This nigga had punked me out of everything that I had, and There wasn't shit that I could do but get the fuck up out of his crib.

I hurried into the bedroom where I had been temporarily sleeping and grabbed what few belongings I had.

I had to get out of Chicago so fast that I wasn't even able to pack a lot of my things. Most of my clothes and possessions were left abandoned at the transitional housing that I moved into after I was released from Lexington House. Since I was keeping small contact with Simone, I asked her to try to get my things from there. She insisted that it would look too suspicious and told me to consider it all a loss since officials at the transitional house considered them abandoned and me a runaway.

Therefore, I had nothing but what I'd picked up here and there while in Minnesota; which was nothing but a cell phone, an iPod, a few outfits, and a few pairs of kicks.

I hurried out of the back door of the basement apartment; praying that them niggas wouldn't change their minds and come after me. Running up on Marlin was a mistake. I didn't know him from Adam, so I damn sure didn't know his willingness to pop me for putting my hands on him.

I felt played as I lightly jogged down the alley. It was cold as fuck outside. I was used to Chicago winters, but Minnesota's cold had an arctic touch to it that was unbearable without layers of long johns and a North Face.

Once I got to the corner, I reached for my phone. There was nobody to call though. I wasn't fucking with a chick that I could go spend the night with. I had no other homeboys.

Without them bricks, I only had a thousand bucks

and nowhere to live. I couldn't afford to rent a room at even the shabbiest motel because I still had to eat. After a week, I would be broke.

I had no other choice; I had to head back to Chicago.

OMARI

After three months, I was finally ready to face Ching. I knew that he wouldn't cop to killing Aeysha, especially at the County during visiting hours with so many guards and listening ears around. I just wanted to be able to look that son of a bitch in his eyes when I told him that I was going to make sure that, if he didn't end up with life for killing Ron Johnson, my intent was on ending his.

I waited along with damn near a hundred other people in a room that smelled like an old basement. The room was filled with young chicks, crying babies, bad ass toddlers, and elderly women with stress in their eyes because they were waiting to see their sons. I was the only person with a lack of remorse or sadness in my expression. I looked like death because I wanted to kill the motherfucker that came walking coolly towards me in a grey jumpsuit.

I guess County food had gotten the best of Ching. He was much slimmer than the last time I saw him. I guess dry ass bologna sandwiches weren't an acquired taste for a punk ass nigga like him.

"Pretty Boy, whad up?"

Ching tried to hide his surprise to see that I was the person there to visit him. It didn't shock me at all that he had the balls to actually sit across from me at the table as if he didn't have a care in the world.

"Funny seeing you here…"

"Cut the bullshit, motherfucka."

Ching slightly laughed at my hostility. Yet, I could see a bit of shock behind his tired and weary eyes. "Damn. You done turned gangsta overnight?"

"You know I never did claim to be a gangsta..."

"But?"

"But you definitely helped turn me into a killa."

Ching tried to act like my words didn't faze him. He tried to continue to sit there looking like he didn't have a care in the world. But I saw it. I saw the worry in the back of his mind that wondered what I was capable of. After Aeysha's murder, I was a different motherfucker. The man that was sitting in front of him wasn't the same nigga that was scared of getting his hands dirty. I was angrier, colder.

He saw that shit.

"What's your point?"

"Point is, if you get off on this murder, it's a bullet on the other side of these walls waiting on yo' ass for killing Aeysha."

There was a possibility that Ching might be released. Word on the street was that his attorney was trying to get the charges dropped because of lack of physical evidence.

Ching's eyes bucked in response to my deadly threat. He snickered, like I was a joke and had nerve to threaten him. Prior to his arrest, Ching had sold drugs for years without much trouble at all. He never had trouble with the law, never got caught for possession. The block boys rarely had trouble. There were robberies here and there, but they got swept under the rug quick by eliminating the problem at the head, like Ching did Ron.

But he'd never had a nigga coming directly at his head.

I planned to be that nigga if he ever saw the free world again.

"Killing Aeysha? Man, I heard rumors that you were putting it in the streets that I killed her, but I never believed it. Nephew…"

I interrupted him by leaning in closely and aggressively whispering, "Don't call me that shit!"

Quickly, I sat back because my suspicious movements caught the attention of one of the guards. Now, I had her full attention, and she was closely watching the exchange between me and Ching.

"Man, dawg, are you serious?" Ching was looking at me like he couldn't believe it. He was putting on a hell of a front.

"Dead serious. You didn't have to kill her. I wasn't gon' say shit. I gave you my word."

I couldn't believe it when he calmly replied, "I know."

This nigga was such a stunt that it wasn't even funny. It disgusted me that he had the balls to kill my woman, but those same balls were nonexistent when it came to fessing up to it.

For weeks he called me a fuck boy and pussy ass nigga because he thought I would crumble under the pressure of the investigation of Ron's murder. But now, here he was acting like a fuck boy when the pussy nigga in me had turned into an animal ready to attack his bitch ass for what he'd done.

"I know I started actin' fucked up towards you when the shit hit the fan about Ron's murder. I said a lot of fucked up shit to you, but it was only to scare you. I wanted to make sure that you wouldn't talk, so I put a little fear in you."

"By killing Aeysha!"

"No. That wasn't me. I ..."

Ching was still talking but I couldn't hear him. The fact that he would fold into a coward was offending the shit outta me. He was tough enough to put me in the middle of a murder. He was heartless enough to kill my woman to keep me quiet. But suddenly he couldn't be a man and tell me to my face that he killed Aeysha.

I'd had enough. I stood from the table and walked away without another word.

I could hear him calling after me. "Nephew! Nephew, come back. Real talk."

But I kept walking. I couldn't afford to get into it with that nigga in that jail. Not only did I want to stay non-confrontational in front of the guards, but I had to remember that I was still an accessory to Ron's murder. If I wanted to stay a free man, I couldn't draw attention to myself by getting into an altercation with Ching.

I knew that, since he had yet to do so, Ching wasn't going to snitch on my involvement in Ron's murder. He lived by a street code so intense that he would do a bid for that murder and allow me to walk the streets free. Unfortunately, it was that same code that made him feel like it was okay to kill the love of my life.

The biting January air outside of the County building smacked me in the face, but it wasn't nearly as cold as my heart. I stuffed my hands in the pockets of my Pelle and braced myself against the strong winds as I walked back to my Challenger with hatred in my heart for the man that practically raised me.

GIA

"This dick feel good to you, baby?"

Rae was panting into my ear while delivering deliberate and extensive strokes inside my tight pussy. Rae was on top of me, missionary style, as my thick chocolate legs spread across the bed, allowing for deeper and more intense penetration.

Rae had forced my arms above my head. To keep me from fighting the dick, Rae's fingers were intertwined amongst mine as I was delivered steady profound strokes that, with a slow rhythm, reached the bottom of my pussy.

"Huh? You like this dick?"

Against my will, I surrendered to Rae's shit talking for the sake of making this fuck session go swift and smooth.

In a flirtatious tone, full of fake moans of pleasure, I allowed, "Yes, baby", to escape my lips as convincingly as I could.

"Tell me how much you like it."

Behind Rae's head, I rolled my eyes. Again, I mustered up the sweetest sexiest voice as I replied, "I don't like it. I *love* it."

"You love me?"

"Of course, I love you."

Those three words were all that Rae needed to hear to just shut up and fuck. She, yes, *she*, then focused on fucking me with the fat eight-inch lambskin strap-on with such intensity that I could swear that she was trying to sexually assault this pussy.

I made a mental note to fake an orgasm in two minutes.

Sex with Rae use to be the bomb. Three years ago, when we met at Sunset, where I dance, the closest I had come to somebody else's pussy was freak shit that I pretended to do on stage with another dancer. Yet, at the age of twenty-two, I was easily persuaded by this smooth soft stud that used her feminine beauty, plus masculine aggression, to turn me into a dyke that catered to her for the next three years.

Rae had been my everything, and I hers. She was a beautiful fair-skinned woman with long locs dyed a dark brownish red. The color popped off her beautifully sculpted face perfectly. She had an awesome body that she often hid under baggy jeans, wife beaters, and Timberlands. Though a beautiful twenty-three year old woman, Rae had turned into a very ugly person over the years.

As a teen, she tried to hide her interest in women. She wasn't open about her interests; even though by looking at her, it was obvious. She wasn't "out". She didn't have gay friends, and she wasn't part of that community. I truly believed that she wasn't comfortable being open about her sexuality because, the one time that she was, she was rejected. Her family disowned her at the age of sixteen, upon her admission of her sexuality and interest in being transgendered. That abandonment, coupled with the confusion of her sexuality, had slowly turned her into an individual that was very insecure, paranoid, and desperate for love.

She was an adoring and loving man trapped in a beautiful woman's body that was madly in love with a woman that had never even been in a lesbian relationship before. All of that ratchetness had taken the spontaneity out of this relationship for me.

I was tired of her insecurities and ready for some real dick.

Finally, I decided that it was time to fake my way out of Rae being on top of me.

"Ooo, shit! I'm cumming," was followed by a bunch of curse words, soft growling, and light scratches on Rae's back until I lay still, huffing and puffing, as if that orgasm took everything out of me. I even made my body convulse suddenly, like the orgasm was still coming down and shocking me.

Rae giggled in delight, kissed me quickly on the lips, and pulled the rubber dick out of me. After unfastening the strap-on and taking it off, she spooned with me so tightly that I could feel her perspiration leaking into my pores. I noticed that, like always, she wasn't holding me in a loving or emotional way. I wasn't lying intimately in her arms. She was holding me captive, wanting to know every time I moved or if I left the bed as she slept.

Just the thought made me laugh at the situation in embarrassing humor.

"What's so funny?"

Instantly, I replied, "Nothing, Rae. Just thought of something."

I could feel her sitting up and, even in the darkness, could see her staring at me. "Thought of what?"

"Nothing, babe."

She grabbed me by the arm and forced me to turn over and look at her. Despite the fact that we were in the darkness, the moonlight shone on her face so I could see the fact that she was actually getting angry.

I smacked my lips and snatched away from her.

"Nothing damn! Go to bed."

She was crazy as hell!

At first, it was cute. At first, Rae's obsessive-compulsive attention and clinginess was perfect. Prior to meeting Rae, I had never been in a relationship that gave me real happiness. My only experience was being with men with no loyalty, honesty, or commitment, who eventually fucked me over to the point of unbelievable heartbreak.

I was born and raised in the Cabrini Green Projects. As soon as I turned eighteen, I started dancing and moved to an apartment complex in Chatham. Living a hard life with niggas whose loyalty was only for the streets, and never for a woman, was embedded in me.

When I met Rae, she was a breath of fresh air. She was the masculinity and protection that my single ass needed. Since she was a woman, she knew exactly what to give me in addition to that; loyalty, affection, and commitment.

In turn, I had given Rae something that she'd never had either: love. I was the family that she got kicked out of. I was the lover that she could never find. I was the friend that she never had because she was so different in a world that didn't understand her.

The more I gave her that love and the more I gave

17

her that family, the more she was erratically intent on keeping it. All while I was seriously ready for yet another breath of fresh air.

Two

SIMONE

I danced in the mirror to "Bad" by Wale that played on the flat screen through one of the U-Verse Music Channels. I switched seductively while swinging twenty-six inches of virgin hair back and forth. I smiled at my reflection as my hands caressed curvaceous hips and squeezed a phat ass. Then I playfully smacked my ass through the True Religion straight legged jeans that I had just squeezed into.

Ever since I got my new body, you couldn't tell me shit. A few weeks after selling my mother's house, I got some injections. I heard one of the girls at Lexington House talking about them. All year, I knew that little heifer had to be stripping or something. There was just no way that a ward of that state could afford the things that she was buying with a McDonald's paycheck.

At any rate, after pulling this so-called top secret information out of her, I hooked up with the fag from Miami that flew to Chicago once a month to give bitches ass and hips in a hotel room somewhere.

Three sessions and forty-five hundred dollars later, I had forty-seven inches of hips and ass.

For years, I'd envied women with curves that kept men at their every beck and call. Finally, I was *that* bitch. After hitting the gym, my body could compete with the best of them. I had the body that I always wanted all of my life and the man of my dreams.

Presently, I was in Omari's bedroom putting the finishing touches on my outfit. I was due to meet him at a bar and grill in Crete for lunch. Even though I'd purchased that condo, soon after Omari and I got together, I started to spend most of my time at his place in Riverdale.

I even had a key.

It's crazy how I never once felt guilty for setting up Aeysha's murder. It was even more insane that the more I settled into this relationship with Omari, the more I was assured that I had done what was best for me.

Finally, I was no longer the side bitch waiting my turn to be in a committed relationship.

As I finished the last touches of my make up, I could hear Dahlia crying in her room. On cue, my eyes rolled and my skin started to crawl.

"Urgh," I groaned as I left the bedroom and walked towards her room to shut her up.

She was wailing and it was so fucking annoying. Omari spoiled this little bitch like she was the next coming of Jesus. Everything was centered around *Dahlia*. Everything was about *Dahlia*. She was the golden child.

Though I'd gotten rid of Aeysha, it was like the bitch was still there! Every time I looked at Dahlia, I saw Aeysha. Not only did Dahlia look just like that bitch, but Omari treated her just like he treated Aeysha. Even though I was his girlfriend, Omari put Dahlia first.

I'd won my man, but I was still sharing him with another bitch!

"Would you shut the fuck up?! Urgh!!" I was livid as I smacked Dahlia out of anger across her little premature leg. I knew that she wasn't big enough for a spanking to get through to her. It just made me feel better to take my anger out on her.

But that only made her go from wailing to straight up hollering.

"Oh, shut up!"

I left the room, figuring that eventually she would shut up or Tiana, the babysitter, would finally arrive so that she could deal with that brat. Tiana was the younger sister of one of the block boys that served for Omari and Capone on the South Side of the city. She was a high school dropout with nothing else to do, so I hired her to babysit. Omari thought that I hired a sitter because I couldn't juggle work while caring for two households and him. That was part of it, but mostly I didn't want to deal with anything that had anything to do with Aeysha, unless it was him.

Just as I was putting my ID and wallet into my Louis Vuitton, above Dahlia's cries, I could hear the doorbell ringing. I grabbed the keys to my Benz, walked passed Dahlia's room, where she was still wailing, and walked towards the front door.

I had been able to upgrade many things since Omari and Capone took over that block on the South Side. After selling my mother's house, giving Chance that twenty-five grand, and splurging a little on myself, I was wearing knockoff bags and barely making the payments on my Camaro. Now I was on Michigan Avenue making high-end purchases with cash.

Omari was far from a kingpin, but he was definitely flipping bricks way faster than he and Capone ever expected.

Once I let Tiana in the house, she heard Dahlia crying and instantly went into Captain-Save-A-Dahlia mode. "Aaaaw! What's wrong with my baby?!"

I didn't even hide the fact that I'd rolled my eyes in

response to Tiana.

"She's fine," I replied, not hiding my irritated tone. "She's probably hungry."

"Does she have bottles in the refrigerator?"

"If Omari left some in there," I replied nonchalantly while going through my purse, looking for some cash to give Tiana.

Tiana giggled before saying, "Miss Simone, don't be treating Dahlia like that."

I smiled, while attempting to hide my hate as Dahlia's cries ricocheted off of the walls. "You know I'm just playing. That's my baby. Mommy just doesn't have time to tend to her. I have to meet her daddy. Speaking of Omari, was he on the block when you left?"

"He left right before me. He said he had to meet you for lunch."

"Okay, well let me get out of here." I handed Tiana fifty dollars before walking out of the door. "I'll be back."

"Take your time."

Just as those slick words left her lips, I stopped in the doorway and turned around to face her little fast ass. "Don't have no niggas in my house."

Tiana couldn't even hide her sly sneaky look. I knew that when she so graciously agreed to babysit for us that she was enjoying the amenities of the house way more than she enjoyed babysitting. We had everything any teenager could dream of; flat screens, stereos, stocked frig, and liquor. I knew that little bitch was drinking. If she was hot enough to hang out on the block and drop out of high school, I didn't put shit past her little ratchet ass.

She stood in the kitchen testing Dahlia's milk on her wrists with a grin on her face that smelled like bullshit. In a synthetic weave, Rainbow jogging suit, and knock off Ugg boots, she looked every bit of ratchet. So I could only imagine what kinda nigga she would have in my house.

"Don't play with me, lil' girl."

"Miss Simone, I am not going to have any company in your house. I promise."

I saw straight through her little ass, but whatever. I couldn't watch her pussy while I was trying to watch mine.

CHANCE

I had been back in Chicago for almost a week.

I stayed in a motel on Cicero Avenue. It was a thirty dollar a night room that was consumed with a stale cigarette smell. I felt like every time I left the room, no matter the amount of cologne I bathed in, the stench of Newports was still on my skin and in my clothes.

Despite the room only being thirty bucks a night, with feeding myself, taking the bus here and there, and copping a good winter coat to do so in, I was down to three hundred dollars.

"Hello?"

Simone sounded irritated when she answered; how she began to sound more and more every time we talked as time went by. I could hear the wind and music in her background. I imagined her riding around careless and worry free. I envied that. While living in Lexington, I feared being on the streets, penniless and homeless. Simone promised that that wouldn't be me, while touching me so intimately that I fell in love with my mentor. I was so in love that I took somebody's life on her behalf.

Despite my loyalty, I still ended up on the streets

penniless and homeless.

Something had gone wrong in a major way.

"I need some cash."

She even laughed at me cynically as she replied, "Okay. And?"

Shortly after killing Aeysha, I started to feel like Simone had set me up. She'd used my naïveté and crush on her to kill somebody that was probably totally innocent. She'd given me this sad story about Aeysha giving her brother the flux with a divorce. She even said that Aeysha was beating her niece.

Funny how I never heard of that brother or niece again after Aeysha was dead.

Either way, that twenty-five thousand sounded damn good regardless of the story behind it.

I can't even act like I wasn't to blame for killing Aeysha. But Simone's complete one-eighty once I killed Aeysha was blowing the fuck outta me.

She'd promised that she was coming to Minnesota. She went as far as to say that she wanted to be with me. She could do that if she left Lexington and came to live with me in Minnesota. She was half the reason why I initially wanted to cop those bricks. On top of needing to flip my cash, I wanted a steady income if she was going to be my lady.

Nevertheless, week after week, she made excuse after excuse as to why she wasn't there yet. Eventually, I figured that she was never coming. Her sudden attitude every time I called further let me know that she'd played me.

"I'm out of cash."

When she heard that I was broke, Simone flipped. "What the fuck?! How?!"

"I was robbed. The nigga I was staying with in Minnesota got me."

Simone growled and moaned like she was so irritated, but I didn't give a fuck. I had done the ultimate for her. She owed me for the rest of her life. I felt like if I called her and told her to jump, her only answer should be 'how high.'

"I'll send you some cash through Western Union."

"You don't have to. I'm in the Chi."

Simone gasped so dramatically that it was slightly funny to me. "Why are you in Chicago?! Are you crazy?!"

"I was popped! I didn't have anywhere to stay. I don't know shit about Minnesota, and I could swear that *somebody* was supposed to be there with me."

Suddenly, Simone's voice went from shit to sugar.

"I know, baby. I couldn't find a job there. I couldn't move there without a job. We would both be broke."

"I thought you still had some dough from selling your mom's crib."

"I do, but I can't live off of that, let alone two people."

I sat on the edge of the bed with my moist forehead in the palm of my hand. Constantly running after Simone mentally was making me drip streams of sweat physically. She was still playing me, but my manhood wouldn't let me concede to that. I was determined to make her keep her end of the bargain. I refused to let the dust of her playing me settle on the surface of this murder.

I eyed the bottle of Grey Goose that sat on the table seducing me. It was looking at me with beautiful, feminine, and seductive glass eyes, licking its intoxicating lips and calling for me.

Simone's empty promises interrupted me and the vodka's flirtation. "Give me a call in a few days. I will see what I can do."

"A few days? I don't have a few days, Simone."

More than needing cash, I had to see her. I hadn't seen her since I left for Minnesota. I had only heard the sound of her voice. Looking into Simone's eyes would tell me if I killed a perfectly innocent woman in exchange for twenty-five thousand dollars and a fuck in the ass.

With sweet convincing words, she told me, "Okay, baby. Call me in two days."

I decided that two days was good enough and hung up. As I hung up, I still had a lot of wonder and questions running marathons in the back of my mind.

I stood up and walked over to the picture window of the ratty motel room while turning up the bottle of Grey Goose. Even the window was filthy with fingerprints and only God knew what else. The lights of Sunset were blinking from across the street. They were calling my name. Luckily, Simone had hooked me up with a fake ID when I left town, so I could get in the club despite being underage.

I touched my pockets. I knew that all I had was a couple hundred dollars that I needed to hold onto just in case Simone flaked on me.

But there was nothing like naked bitches twerking in g-strings to make a nigga feel better.

GIA

♫ *Okay, Southside I gotta own this, snakeskin on my hat,*
albino
I'm rich, like Lionel, I get head like Rhino
I'm riding on my rivals, survival, viable
Blindfold, bullets, for y'all niggas?

I got extra
I got extra
I got money
I got work for his hoes
I got a plethora ♫

I was currently hanging upside down on the stainless steel pole in six-inch heels twerking remarkably to "Extra" by 2 Chainz. I was a perfectionist when it came to stripping, and I was one of the most sought after dancers in Sunset.

Unlike many dancers who had asses and hips injected full of saline and breasts full of silicone, I was all natural. I didn't have a big stupid ass booty or huge perky breasts. I was a petite 5'4" with a runner's body. My ass was big enough. My breasts were luscious enough. My waist was invisible. With dark skin like a Haitian and a long Malaysian weave that fell twenty-eight inches from my scalp, I was *living* as I hung upside down clapping my ass.

My pole skills were serious. I twirled, spun, and flipped like every dollar depended on it, because it did. I climbed all the way to the top of the pole. Up there, near the roof, I was able to see the patrons on the second floor balcony. They catcalled over 2 Chainz' ratchetness. Dollar bills floated into the air and rained all over me. I recognized a few of the partiers. I smiled to acknowledge them before sliding down the pole at record speed and landing in a split at the bottom of the pole so hard that you would think that it hurt. My heels hit the floor of the stage with a loud clunk.

Sunset was a nude strip club. Therefore, as many men made it rain, hundreds of George Washington's kissed my skin and stuck to me.

Since it was a Saturday night, the club was packed to capacity. Money was definitely in the building. I recognized a lot of well known dope dealers. They were real hustlers; not just dudes who stood on the block and sold weed, but men who pushed weight and drove hundred thousand dollar luxury vehicles. Luckily, I was the favorite of many of them. They stood at the stage throwing band after band of singles and five dollar bills. Some of them gave their lady a band to make it rain on me.

Strip clubs had become such an acceptable pastime that half of the patrons in attendance were women. They stood amongst the tight crowd at the front of the stage waving dollars in the air, beckoning for me to crawl over to them and pop my pussy in their faces.

Rae was also in the crowd sipping, lingering, and watching – like always. She often patronized the club. She got VIP treatment when she was at Sunset because the bouncers, bartenders, and owners knew that she was Gia's woman, one of the most popular dancers.

As I positioned myself on all fours and twerked my ass in some girl's face with a birthday crown on, I could see Rae sitting at a table in the farthest corner, cuddling a Corona in one hand and a double shot of Patron in the other. Her eyes were glassy as she stared at me intensely. The way she watched me was starting to get scary; as if she knew I was going to leave her any day now.

Unfortunately, she was absolutely correct.

I just didn't know when. But what I did know was that her intense look was the start of some bullshit later on that night.

The eyes of someone else caught my attention as well. They weren't on me and that bothered me. They weren't on any other stripper and that intrigued me. With a tall lanky stature and locs that hit his shoulders, he sat hovering over a bottle. Many naked women walked by him propositioning him. Yet, he nicely rejected their advances for lap and private dances and put his focus back on his date, Don Julio.

2 Chainz finally stopped talking shit, so I began to quickly pick up the dollar bills that covered the stage like carpet. Reese, a bouncer, used a broom to quickly assist me as the next dancer came to the stage already popping her ass as Lil' Wayne's high pitched voice came spilling from the speakers accompanied with a sick bass line.

I stuffed what I estimated to be about five hundred dollars in the Michael Kors book bag that I used to house my tips. I had already grossed over a thousand dollars in tips and it was only midnight.

Carefully, I tipped off the stage with Reese's assistance.

It was pitiful the way that Rae broke her neck to catch my eye. I knew that she was trying to get my attention, but I was focused on getting this money. She was really starting to blow me with the way she wanted to walk me around on this leash. She was losing her edge. Everything that led me to fall for her in the first place was evaporating before my eyes.

I ignored the way Rae broke her neck to get my attention. I knew that I would hear about that later, but I didn't give a fuck. I was there to work, not babysit her insecurities.

With interest, I walked over to the guy spooning with the Don Julio bottle. Along the way, I reserved a few offers for lap dances for later that night.

"Hey you." I spoke seductively as I slid my arm around his muscular shoulders. Despite being lanky, his arms and shoulders were muscular as if he did pushups.

Initially, he nonchalantly glanced at me while replying halfheartedly. "Whad up?"

His lack of attention made me force myself on him. I sat across from him at his table, took his bottle, and poured myself a drink. He looked curiously at my nerve. I was so bold that he had to laugh as he looked at my teasing smile.

I was daring him to have a problem with me drinking from his bottle.

"You're welcome," he said with a laugh.

"I know I am," I said, still smiling as I took the shot. "What's your name?"

For the first time that night, I saw him smile. He

met my fun smile, which I gave him as an attempt to get him out of his funk.

Finally he answered, "My name is Chance."

THREE

GIA

By five o'clock the next morning, I definitely paid for ignoring Rae's attempts to get my attention.

She yelled and banged her hands against the steering wheel as she drove at eighty miles an hour down 94-West. "You treat me like shit, and I don't like it! Respect me, man!"

We were in a heated discussion as we rode home in her 2013 blacked out Tahoe.

"What the fuck do you want me to do, Rae?! I'm a stripper! It's my job to talk to people and get money. Not talk to yo' ass all night!"

"But you can talk to that nigga all night?!"

"What nigga?!"

I was playing dumb, but I knew who she was talking about. She was talking about Chance. Without even thinking, I'd spent nearly two hours at his table. We drank and talked shit. It wasn't on purpose. Somehow, I was just drawn into him. Chance had such an interesting story. I'm sure the Don Julio was to blame for his openness, but he was so up front with how broke he was and that he was currently homeless and living out of a motel.

He said that he'd just moved to Chicago from Minnesota. He'd bought two bricks to flip and his roommate robbed him. He grew up as a ward of the state. Therefore, he didn't have any family to run to when he was forced to leave Minnesota for the same reasons.

That's a story you don't hear every day. In a strip club, men give you the same story; crazy baby mama, nagging wife, rich dope boy, or rap star dreams. I was so drawn into the difference in this young cutie that I regretfully forgot that my "security" was watching me.

"You know what nigga I'm talking about! Don't play with me!" Rae was so angry that she was gritting her teeth while giving me her full attention, not the road. The truck began to swerve out of our lane.

"Rae, pay attention to the road!"

She ignored me, continuing to glare at me with fire in her eyes. She was so upset that her pale skin was turning red. "Who is he?!"

"I don't know him!"

"WHO THE FUCK IS HE?!"

The driver of the car passing us on our left blew the

horn because Rae damn near collided with him. She finally took control of the steering wheel and gave the road her full attention.

"Are you seriously arguing with me over a nigga at the club?! You've got to be kidding me!" Tears were in my eyes. "I can't do this shit no more!"

Officially, I was done. There was no use in staying in this relationship any longer. I was unhappy, and Rae did nothing to make it any better. Rae was too fucking delusional. No matter what, we would consistently end up in arguments like this because there was something wrong in her that I could not fix, nor was I willing to.

She had some serious mental issues that needed professional help.

Rae saw my tears, and she knew. She saw my surrender towards this relationship. At five in the morning, with the feeling of dollar bills still against my skin, with the stench of smoke still in my hair, I was so done with this relationship. Chance showed me that. I didn't even know him. But as he sat there and told me that he was broke and homeless, I envied him. I was willing to give anything to be in his position, rather than feeling Rae's burning brown eyes glaring at me from the corner like a pedophile. Though broke and homeless, Chance was free to change his life for the better, to move about life without somebody weighing him down.

Though far from broke or homeless, I didn't have those options because I felt chained to somebody.

As Rae got off of the expressway and went west on Eighty-Seventh Street, I noticed that she hadn't responded to me. Suddenly, her hostility was out of the window. Suddenly, she was passive, not aggressive. That assured me even more that I was done. The way that she flipped so quickly showed me how she so pathetically needed me. She held onto this relationship so tight, not because she loved me or wanted to be my partner, but because she didn't know how to be herself without me.

That was a dangerous situation that I no longer wanted to be a part of.

"Rae, we need some space."

Usually I just dealt with her instability because I felt sorry for her. But, finally, I felt sorry for myself.

"I'm not happy. I haven't been for a long time. I'm tired of arguing. I'm tired of explaining myself. I need some space."

"Just like that?"

I met her eyes. When I saw that we both had tears slowly flowing down our beautiful feminine faces, I realized that we were two very confused and lost women that needed time apart to figure things out.

"Yes. Just like that."

Just as the words left my lips, Rae pulled up in front of our house on Princeton. I hopped out of the car before she could say whatever it was that her tears were planning to say. I was tired, sleepy and very ready to sleep freely, not with my insecure girlfriend holding me in a bear hug all night.

"Can we talk about this?"

The way she begged made my skin crawl. I walked into the house wondering how truly confused she had to be to be a woman dressed like a man acting like such a pussy.

"No. I don't feel like talking, Rae. It's five o'clock in the morning and I just want to get some sleep." As I walked into the house and into the living room, I threw my duffle bag onto the floor. Then I told Rae, "Sleep on the couch."

"What?!"

She was behind me before I knew it, grabbing my arms so tight that my bones crunched in her tight grip.

"Let me go!"

I fought to get away. She fought to keep me in her grasp. I began to swing as much as I could, which wasn't much.

"You just gone leave me like this?! It's that easy?!"

"Let me go, Rae!"

"Is it somebody else? Who you fuckin'?!"

I couldn't believe this bitch. I looked at her like she was crazy as I fought to get out of her grip. "Let me go, bitch!"

"Who is he?!"

It was funny how Rae instantly assumed that this somebody else was a he.

Just to be catty, I replied, "None of your fucking business! Now what?!"

Bam!

Her fist made rapid and hard contact with my eye. I fell to my knees, allowing a sharp cry to escape my lips as I held my eye with both hands. The punch hurt, but the fact that she hit me hurt much worse. I had never been hit before in my life, and for the first time to be with my live-in lesbian lover was further proof that my love life needed a renovation.

I could hear Rae apologizing over and over again. I could hear her beginning to cry. I could feel her hovering over me, attempting to gently stand me up.

"Get the fuck the out!"

"Baby..."

"Get the fuck out!! NOW!"

I don't know if she realized how bad she had just fucked up or if she was listening to my anger, but she walked away without another word or any further argument. As I held my throbbing and swelling eye, I watched her solemnly walk out of the living room and towards the front door. The closer she got to the door, the more weight left my shoulders.

As I heard the door open and close, it was amazing how, even with indescribable pain in my face, I felt the freest I had felt in years.

SIMONE

"What is this bruise on her leg?"

Blood rushed from my head as I strapped myself into the passenger seat of Omari's car. While strapping Dahlia into her car seat in the back, Omari continued to question me. "Did you see this?"

I had. I noticed the bruise on Dahlia's leg that morning as I watched Omari bathe her in her tub. I logged a mental note not to smack her anymore.

"No, babe. I hadn't noticed. What kind of bruise?"

"I don't know. I can't tell. Her little leg is just red and purple." Suddenly, he was cooing all in Dahlia's face. It was so hard for me to hide my repulsion. However, I hurried up and fixed my face after hearing him close the back door. Soon, he was climbing into the driver's seat.

"I'm gone have to ask Tiana about that shit."

I played dumb. "About what?"

"That bruise on my baby's leg!" His face was balled up with irritation as he backed out of the driveway. "She needs to watch her more carefully. I don't play that shit when it comes to my baby."

I slid my hand on his thigh. "Baby, calm down. A toy probably hit her or something in her crib."

Omari agreed as jealousy boiled in my stomach.

I couldn't remember Omari ever being that upset about anything regarding me.

We were on our way to his sister's house in Indianapolis for dinner. I wasn't about to nitpick and make the three hour drive unbearable.

However, for the entire two hours and fifty-seven minutes that it took to get to Erica's house, he talked about Dahlia. He groveled over how little and precious she was, how beautiful she was, how much she looked like Aeysha, yadda, yadda, yadda. He never mentioned how good I looked in my faux leather jogger suit. He never mentioned how good the Chanel No. 5 smelled on my skin. Compared to Dahlia, I wasn't even in the fucking car.

I zoned out completely. I stared out of the window, putting all of my tension into biting the acrylic nail on my thumb. That feeling of being second best was nauseatingly sitting in the pit of my stomach.

As yet another call from Chance flashed on my iPhone screen that was on silent, the tension became so much worse. Chance had been straight blowing my phone up since he got back to Chicago. I had to think of something fast to get him off of my tail. I couldn't be attached to him in any way, shape, or form. I thought sending him to Minnesota would work, but he was even too stupid to flip a brick! Who runs through twenty-five grand with nothing to show for it?!

Urgh!

I couldn't afford to give Chance anything more than what I owed him. I gave Omari the money he needed to set up the blocks on the South Side with Capone. He did give it back once money started to be made, but it was in my savings, which I was not about to touch. If I ever came up in the investigation of Aeysha's murder, I needed that savings just in case I had to go on the run.

Besides, Chance and I had a deal. I kept my end of the bargain. He wasn't about to blackmail me because he was irresponsible with twenty-five thousand dollars. He could kiss my ass for all I cared.

I stared out of the window hypnotically, randomly responding to Omari as if I was listening, until we pulled up in front of Erica and her husband's home. It was beautiful and huge; more than six thousand square feet. Since it was a waterfront home, there was a deeded boat dock in the back that could clearly be seen from the driveway. This was a home easily worth more than a million dollars.

"Wow. This is nice."

As he pulled into the driveway, Omari replied, "Yeah. Her husband bought this house after he got some gig out here. This motherfucka nice."

This would be Omari's first time seeing his sister in about five years. He had never even met Erica's husband that she married at a courthouse ceremony. Erica was Omari's older sister and only sibling. They didn't have the same father. They grew up on different sides of town, because she was raised by her dad, who had an estranged relationship with their mother. Due to constant fights between Omari's mother and Erica's father, Erica and Omari had been pretty estranged their whole life. It wasn't until Aeysha was killed that Erica reached out to him. Now, they were attempting to mend their relationship, especially since Erica was about two months pregnant with Omari's first niece or nephew.

Erica excitedly opened the door before we could even ring the doorbell.

I was immediately taken aback by her beauty. Her resemblance to Omari was uncanny. She had those signature gray eyes, and her physical appearance was just as stunning as Omari's. She had such dark and gorgeous features that she looked exotic; almost Indian.

"Hi! Oh my God! I'm so happy to see you!"

Despite Omari carrying Dahlia in her car seat, Erica threw her arms around Omari.

Omari smiled happily. To give them room to embrace, I took Dahlia out his arms and he then was able to wrap his arms around his sister.

I couldn't help but take in the ambiance of this crib! The twelve foot ceilings were overwhelming. The view of the lake out of the picture window was amazing.

Erica had definitely married well.

"Let me get a picture," I heard a familiar voice from my past say in the distance. The familiarity hit me so hard that I damn near dropped Dahlia.

I looked up and locked eyes with Tre, who looked disgusted to see me.

Just looking at him brought back awful memories of last year. Looking him in the eyes so vividly reminded me of how I practically begged him to stay with me, to choose me over his wife. Chills ran down my spine as I remembered him literally fighting to get away from me and treating me like a disposable whore ever since.

"Baby, this is my brother, Omari, and his girlfriend, Simone." Erica was so happy that she didn't even notice the tension in Tre's face.

On cue, I smiled and reached out to shake his hand.

"Hello, Tre. Nice to meet you."

"You too," he barely said. He instantly switched his focus to Omari. His tone totally changed when speaking to him. "What's up, Omari? I heard so much about you, man!"

Again, no one noticed the tension. Omari was shaking it up with Tre and Erica was busy getting Dahlia out of her chair. But me? Despite a cool exterior, I was boiling on the inside. So this was the wife? *This* was the bitch that was better than me? This was the bitch that had him treating me like yesterday's trash?

Unlike my other significant others, Tre wasn't into social media. He didn't have a Facebook page, Instagram, or Twitter. Therefore, I wasn't as able to find out about his wife or how she looked like I did Aeysha. He was always very discreet about his wife, never giving me any details about her. Like Omari, I had done a background check on Tre to find out where he lived. I knew that his wife's name was Erica, but the fact that his wife and Omari's sister were one in the same was blowing me away.

After meets and greets, we settled on an antique couch in a large living room. Again, I zoned out. I stared into the sixty inch flat screen that silently played a rerun of Scandal. Like Olivia Pope, once again I was being the good little mistress that kept my relationship with my lover well hidden. I sat there and listened to Tre overtly boast about how beautiful his wife was, how much he loved her, and how perfect their life was. I knew that each word was said with the intention of stabbing me in my broken heart. I should have been able to sit there and do the same. I had finally won. I finally had my own man. But in that living room, I felt like a fifth wheel. The four of them – Tre, Erica, Omari, and Dahlia – they were family and connected by something that only Aeysha would have ever been able to fit in.

"So, Simone," Erica said getting my attention as she sat beside me. Omari and Tre had started an intense conversation about the NBA playoffs, so I guess Erica was ready to pay me some attention. "This is my first baby, so I want to know from somebody with experience. I know you didn't give birth to Dahlia, but how is it raising a baby?"

I bit my tongue. I swallowed the disgust. I fought the urge to roll my eyes. I smiled perfectly and said, "Oh I love it. It's like she's mine. The circumstances were unfortunate, but she is a good baby. I don't have any children, so it's like a blessing in disguise."

Erica was saying some sappy shit about being pregnant for the first time and how when it was my turn I would love it, but I barely heard her. Tre's voice overrode hers. I could hear him excusing himself to the kitchen.

I waited a few minutes before asking Erica, "Where is your restroom?"

"Oh, I'll show you! Come on."

"No," I insisted. "I can find my way. Talk to your brother. It's been a long time. Get as much in before Tre comes back and basketball takes over."

She gave me quick directions to the restroom. I disappeared down a long hallway and followed the sounds of Tre, who was in the kitchen stirring a pot of what smelled like spaghetti.

"So that's her?"

It's like Tre knew I was coming. The sound of my voice didn't scare, move, or faze him.

He continued stirring the pot while saying, "Get the fuck out, bitch."

"It's like that?"

"It's been like that. Now get the fuck out, before I put yo' ass out."

He didn't scare me, not in his house anyway. I knew that he wouldn't get loud or put his hands on me with his wife a few feet away.

With a smirk, I said, "She's pretty."

"She's *beautiful*. Way more beautiful than you."

That's when his eyes met mine. He looked at me with eyes that dismissed everything I thought I stood for. When I thought I existed, his eyes told me that I was nothing. "*Get. The. Fuck. Out.*"

His threatening words didn't scare me away, but the way he looked at me like I was the scum of the earth did.. His dismissive glare brought back familiar feelings that I'd worked damn hard to get rid of.

OMARI

"Whad up, Capone?"

I took Capone's call in the front yard of Erica's crib. The living room was thick with conversation about relationships, marriages, and babies. Simone was all too involved with the conversation and was way too eager to involve me, so I was happy to have a reason to get the fuck out of there.

It's not like I didn't want to marry Simone. It's not like I didn't want another baby eventually. But Simone had always been very pressed on both issues. She went from finally being my woman to picking out wedding rings in the blink of an eye. I wasn't ready for either. I was finally getting my life back on track. I was finally able to look at my baby and not burst into tears with thoughts of Aeysha. I was finally able to fuck Simone without feeling guilty.

A baby and marriage was nowhere in the cards anytime soon.

"Got some bad news for you."

"Talk to me."

I braced myself. Capone's bad news could only be one of two things, both having to do with work. Anything to do with my drugs and bad news had a lot to do with either the police or a nigga robbing us.

"Ching's case got dropped."

But I was never expecting that.

"*THE FUCK*?!"

"I know, man."

"Are you sure?!" Spit was flying from my mouth and my jaws clinched with fury as I spoke through gritted teeth.

"I swear. That nigga is home. Case was dropped yesterday on a technicality. No body and not enough evidence."

This couldn't be real. As I ended the call, sorrow took over me like the day I saw Aeysha's heart stop beating. I knew that Ching was in jail for killing Ron, but, because he was in jail, I felt like God was making a way for him to pay for Aeysha's death too. Those bars rescued him from my wrath. Those bars were his protection. Now on the other side of those bars, it was my duty to kill this nigga. No, I wasn't a street nigga. Capone had to spend months showing me the ropes on this drug shit. But I didn't need him to show me how to be a cold-hearted killer. Every time I thought about Ayesha being taken from me by anyone's hands but God's, being a killa was an instant persona that consumed the blood that flowed through me.

FOUR

OMARI

Two days later, I was in my living room ready to make Ching pay for killing Aeysha.

"You know if we do this, you're starting a war, right?"

I looked at Capone peculiarly. "*We*?"

Sarcastically, Capone laughed while licking the swisher that he'd just finished rolling full of the best loud we'd put on the streets since we set up camp on the South Side.

After successfully licking the swisher closed airtight, he told me, "Yea, *we*. You think I'm gon' let you do this shit by yourself?"

I smiled on the inside. No matter how young Capone was, he had been loyal than a motherfucka since we linked up.

Since copping from Ching's connect three months ago, Capone and I had successfully set up a trap house over east on Seventy-Ninth Street. We were flipping about three bricks a week. Mollies sold like crazy. In that three months, I was able to give Simone back the money she loaned me to cop. That was the first thing on my to-do list. Now, I was back to the regularly scheduled program; living, shopping, taking care of my family, and paying off mom's crib.

Though Capone certainly put in more work in the streets since he was more knowledgeable, he treated me more like his boss then his partner. I guess because I was older than him and put in more bread than him, he gave me that respect.

"Besides, I think Ching foul as hell. He went too far."

Capone looked at me cautiously. He knew that the subject of conversation was super sensitive for me. Just referring to Ching killing Aeysha set me off. But this kind of conversation was different. I was rectifying the situation, not mourning it.

"I'm riding with you all the way, homie. But are you sure?"

It was no question. Ching had fucked up my entire life, and even my daughter's. Yes, I was still living, but I was a shell of the man that I once was. I was raising my daughter and living life, but it was all in a daze. All of my unconditional happiness for life was buried with Aeysha. I made good money. I had a beautiful daughter and a loyal woman. But none of that was able to fill a void that I walked around with every day.

If I had to live with this feeling of death every day, then it was only fair that the motherfuckas responsible for it felt it too.

"It's no question."

Capone sat back and pulled on the blunt. He stared into the air as if he was letting this all sink in. It was definitely something to meditate on. We were about to go to war with the man we used to work for, with the man that raised both of us.

"Just Ching?"

"Smoke, Black, and Bert too. Ching was in jail when Aeysha got killed, so he had to have one of them niggas do it."

A noise could be heard in the hallway before Capone could respond. We quickly quieted our scheming until the coast was clear.

Eventually, the rumbling in the hallway stopped, but Capone still leaned in and spoke in a much lower tone. "So how we gon' do this? You just trying to pop these niggas or what? They can't be hard to find."

"No. When I say war, I mean war. I'm going

through they spots and taking shit. I'm causing a drought. I'm shooting up blocks… *Then* I'm killing them niggas."

SIMONE

I was pissed. Both Tre and Omari could kiss my ass with their undying devotion to these hoes.

My fingers pounded on the keyboard like stiletto heels on pavement. I was livid. I typed Tre a lengthy email full of hatred towards his smug ass, his "precious wife", and their bound to be funny looking bundle of joy.

Further irritation began to make my blood boil as Chance continuously blew my phone up, as he had been doing for the past few days. He was getting restless. I figured it was time to do something.

Just as I clicked the send button in the Gmail window, I heard the ADT system chirp, signaling that the front door was opening. I broke my neck to leave the computer desk in the office and get to the window. Sure enough, Capone was leaving.

I marched out of the office and down the hallway. Rage was flowing from me so much that my skin felt hot with anger.

This was never going to end. He was always going to love Aeysha. She would always be a permanent fixture in our relationship.

"So, you're willing to go to jail for her?"

My words shocked Omari, who was sitting coolly on the couch clicking through the Comcast channels.

"What are you talking about?"

"Ching! You're about to kill him, Omari! Are you serious?!"

Instead of anger, I showed him hurt. I showed him a distraught woman that was tired of playing second to a woman that wasn't even there anymore.

With tears in my eyes, I stood in the entryway of the living room portraying a broken heart rather than a vengeful killer. "You're willing to kill Ching and end up in jail for the rest of your life?! What about me and Dahlia?! What are we suppose to do? What if his boys try to retaliate and kill you? What if I end up like Aeysha?! Did you think about that?!"

His heart went out to my tears. He stood from the couch and walked towards me as I stood in the entryway wiping away my distressed tears that were cloudy with Estee Lauder foundation.

When he tried to put his arms around me, I smacked his arms away.

"No! Tell me that you aren't going to kill him. Promise me!"

He didn't promise me. As a matter of fact, he didn't say anything. He just stood there, slipping his hands into the pockets of his True Religion jeans, and giving me the same disdain look that he gave me back when he told me that he was never leaving Aeysha.

"You're so worried about avenging her death, but what about me?! What about me as I raise your daughter and hold you down? WHAT ABOUT ME?!"

Anger sent me flying back down the hallway, stomping like a heavy woman. On the inside, I scolded myself for not being better, for not being good enough to take his mind off of her. But on the outside I cried sad and sorrowful tears.

Omari came after me. He entered the office right after me and put his arms around me.

Omari kissed my cheek. When his lips left my face, they were wet with my tears.

"I'm sorry, baby," he told me as he wiped my face with the palm of his hands. "I was with her seven years though. That's the mother of my child. I can't let him get away with it. I can't look at Dahlia every day knowing that I didn't do shit about her mother's murder. I would do the same for you."

CHANCE

After calling Simone's cell with no answer for days, there was finally a knock on my motel room door.

I figured it was her. She was the only person that knew what room number I was in. I'd given it to her a few days ago when she was suppose to be bringing me some bread.

My cash was dwindling fast. Soon, I wouldn't be able to afford to pay for the shitty hotel that I was staying in. I had barely eaten anything that day. I had even resorted to looking for a job because things were getting so tight.

We had to do something. I was in this predicament strictly because of Simone and she was gone fix this shit.

When I opened the door, this bitch had the nerve to smile at me. I couldn't believe the size balls this bitch had. It was crazy how just last year, I was drooling over her, ready to kill and did kill for her, and now, when I laid eyes on her, I questioned her sanity.

She had to be crazy to think that there was anything to smile about.

I turned around and left her standing in the doorway.

"Urgh. Well, hello to you too, Chance."

This was my first time seeing her since the day I left for Minnesota. She'd changed in ways that money could only help somebody change. Her hair was expensive. Her clothes were luxury. I recognized the Lexus keys and new body.

"Murder looks damn good on you."

She stood leaning against the desk as I sat on the bed. She had the nerve to give me this flirtatious smile. It was the same smile that I use to fall for.

"You got some money?"

She looked hurt that I got straight to the point.

"Chance." She was sweetly singing my name in a flirtatious moan as she switched towards me. Then Simone sat beside me on the bed; immediately laying her soft hands on my exposed leg. She pushed my basketball shorts up until my dick fell out of them.

"Naw." I shook my head and immediately pushed her away. That was the bullshit she'd done to sway me in the first place; grabbing my dick, holding me, and touching me like she was going to eventually give me the pussy. "Don't try to play me, man!!"

"Chance, calm down."

Anger consumed me so much that I jumped to my feet. "Naw, fuck that! I'm starving, man. I'm out here in these streets with nothing while you driving clean and rocking fucking Gucci bags!" I smacked her purse so hard that it fell off of the coffee table and onto the floor. "Stop playing with me! I killed that…"

"Shut up!" Suddenly, Simone looked possessed. She jumped to her feet and stood staring me face to face. Her eyes popped out of her head and her jaws clenched. She was no longer the sweet chick willing to fuck me. She was the vicious bitch that planned a murder with me. That's the bitch I wanted to see because that's the bitch that owed me, more than money, but her life, cause I put mine on the line for her.

"Be quiet before somebody hears you! These damn walls are thin as paper."

I slowed down. I didn't want to piss her off so bad that she went home without giving me some money. I eased up. I played her role. I played it phony. "What am I suppose to do, Simone? I'm broke."

After picking up her purse from the floor, she reached in it and handed me an envelope.

"How much is this?"

She nonchalantly replied, "A thousand dollars."

My heart sank. With disgust, I threw the envelope on the bed. "I can't live off of this."

"What do you expect me to do? I gave you twenty-five thousand dollars, Chance!"

"Them niggas stole my shit!" I was damn near in tears. I couldn't do shit with a grand but live for another month.

I was straight. Before I killed Aeysha, I was good. Though I was broke and unhappy in transitional housing, I had a free roof over my head that I stupidly gave away because this bitch promised me twenty-five grand attached to a future with her.

"I don't have anything to do with that. We had a deal and I fulfilled my end of the bargain."

"Really, you didn't," I told her as I walked towards her. Poking her in her chest as I pointed at her, I added, "You never came to Minnesota."

"I had to find a job! Apparently that was a must since you couldn't flip twenty-five grand!"

"So that's it? You just gone leave me out here like this? Where am I suppose to live? I can't even go back to transitional housing."

"I don't know. I'll think of something."

That sounded like a lie.

I looked over her expensive attire and jewelry and knew that she had to be living somewhere comfortably.

"Why can't I come stay with you?"

"Chance, I wish you could. I really do. I hate seeing you in this motel," she said frowning in disgust as she looked around. "But we cannot be linked together in this city."

"They aren't even investigating her murder."

"The investigation is still ongoing, Chance. Whether they have any leads is a different story."

Simone continued to fill the stale cigarette poisoned air with lies. As she promised me that she would fix everything, that she would help me find a job and a place to stay, I saw straight through her lies. This bitch had played me. Every second that this realization danced at the forefront of my mind, I felt stupid as hell.

She even hugged me and told me that everything would be okay, while also saying that she had to leave. She had to leave and go get in her fancy car and go to what was most likely a nice warm crib while I sat in that motel room figuring out how the fuck I was going to eat.

GIA

"Hello?"

I was standing in the mirror in the dressing room taking singles from various places on my body and putting them inside of my Michael Kors book bag that I planned to lock inside of my locker.

After checking my cell phone and seeing that I missed five of Rae's call, I decided to call her back.

Things had been great for the past few days. Rae was staying in a hotel and begging me to let her come back home. I wasn't budging. I felt the best that I had felt in years. I felt free and like I could do what the fuck I wanted to. I was given the space to realize that I didn't want Rae anymore.

She'd given me the best excuse to use to leave this relationship when she hit me.

She had the nerve to greet me like nothing was wrong. "Hey, baby."

Instantly, my eyes rolled into the back of my head as I fixed my hair in the full length mirror.

"What's up, Rae? I'm at work," I spoke dryly.

"Why are you acting like this?"

"Like what?"

"Like you don't give a fuck about me anymore."

"I give a fuck about you."

"Then let me come back home."

"Now *that* is what I don't give a fuck about."

After smacking her lips and sighing dramatically, Rae swore, "I am so sorry, baby. I can't believe I put my hands on you."

"Rae, I have to go…"

I could hear her tears beginning to flow as she replied, "Please forgive me, baby…"

"I have to go, Rae."

I ended the call before she could say anything else, threw my iPhone in my locker, along with my tips, and locked the combination lock.

Though it was a Tuesday night, the club was still thick with niggas, bitches, money, and smoke. I'd just gotten off of the stage, so I was working the crowd when I spotted the same guy that I chatted it up with last week that got me socked in the eye.

Rae punched me because I had the nerve to talk to another man in her face. She can act like it was because I was talking about leaving her, but I knew better.

For the first time in our relationship, it appeared as

if I was into somebody else. And for the first time in our relationship, she hit me. Two plus two equals a jealous bitch.

I could still feel the soreness around my eye. Thankfully, no remnants of the black eye could be seen through a hell of a lot of concealer and Mac Studio Fix.

"Hey you."

When Chance looked up at me, it took him a minute to recognize me.

"Gia," I reminded him.

"Oh, yea! What's up, girl? You here to drink up some more of my liquor?"

As I took it upon myself to rest my butt in the only other seat at his table, I replied jokingly, "Oh, you're too kind! Thanks for offering."

FIVE

CHANCE

Everything was a blur. After two bottles of Don Julio, I could barely see straight as me and Gia left the truck stop.

I thought that putting food on my stomach would sober me up. But as I slid into the passenger seat of her 300, I fought the urge to throw up. Gia was pretty fucked up too. I could feel the car swerving a little bit as she jumped on the e-way.

"You need me to drive?"

She looked at me like I was out of my mind. "Yea right. I'm not trying to die tonight." Then she giggled.

Gia was fine as hell. That's all I thought about all night as I let her drink up most of my gawd damn liquor. I hadn't chilled with a female in a long time. Since killing Aeysha, most of my time had been consumed with laying low and figuring out how I was going to live.

Not only was Gia gorgeous, but she had good conversation. Unfortunately, I was always so drunk when I talked to her that I told her all of my business. Surprisingly, after finding out how broke, homeless, and fucked up I was, she kept talking to me and chilled with me even longer this time around. That night, she drank for fun, but I was drinking out of anger. I enjoyed Gia's company, but thoughts of Simone were playing over and over again in my mind like a movie. Every time I remembered her smiling and flirting with me, I took a shot. Every time I thought about her convincing me how Aeysha needed to be killed, I took a shot. Every time I remembered hearing Aeysha's pregnant and blood curdling screams, I took a shot. I wondered if her baby lived, and I took a double shot.

I was fucked up.

"We're closer to my crib than yours. I am barely making it," Gia confessed while fighting hard to keep the car from swerving into the next lane.

"I told you I could drive."

"And I said I wanted to live. Do you have to go home tonight?"

"To the motel? Hell naw."

We both laughed.

"Cool. We're going to my crib then."

That didn't sound bad at all. I was so ready to sleep in a bed with a soft mattress. Hell, she could have put me on the couch for all I gave a fuck. It would have been better than that bullshit bed that I had been sleeping in for two weeks.

However, when we got to her crib on the Southwest side, she didn't make me sleep on the couch. She led me through the house by the hand, but we both kept each other from falling over our drunken feet. It was six in the morning. The sun was coming up. So once she got in the bedroom, I was able to peep a few pictures of her and another nigga... or a chick... I couldn't really tell since I was so wasted. But then she drew the curtains that totally blocked out the sun.

She threw me off when she began to take her clothes off. I figured she was too drunk to realize that she was about to sleep in her underwear next to a complete stranger.

When I lay down fully dressed, she shrieked. "Uh huh! Get out of my bed in them clothes you been keeping in that nasty ass motel."

I laughed. "Damn, it's like that?"

"Yup," she said with a laugh. "Take them clothes off."

As I stripped, I told her, "I can sleep on the couch, you know."

"Boy, you already been sleeping in a motel. Enjoy

this bed while you can."

I was all too prepared to go to sleep. I wasn't even trying to push up on shorty. But as soon as we lay down, she spooned with me. She laid across my chest and wrapped her leg around mine. Instantly, my dick got hard and lay up against her leg.

With a flirtatious giggle, she asked, "Damn. That's all you?"

I matched her giggle. "What's that mean?"

In response, she took her hand and rubbed it up and down my dick.

"Gawd damn," slipped from her mouth.

She was drunk. I knew it. But I also knew that I had never had anyone as beautiful as she was ever this close to me. I didn't fight her. I let the liquor persuade her to do whatever she wanted to do to me.

Suddenly, my dick was her playground. It wasn't even about me. She saw the dick and just wanted it. She jagged it and played with it like it was a new toy. I just lay there trying to sober up enough to fuck her if that's what she wanted.

For the second time in twenty-four hours, a bad ass chick was trying to feel my dick. I was actually feeling this chick, though. I hadn't had pussy in forever, so when Gia went from playing with it to sucking it, I fought the urge to bust too quickly in her mouth.

SIMONE

I sat on my bed in my condo trying to stop the tears.

I stared in disbelief at the email from Tre displayed in the Gmail app in my iPhone. He'd told me time and time again that he loved his wife. He told me time and time again that he would never be with me. Our time had ended, and I was now with somebody that loved me. But reading the words that day still hurt because behind the extensions, behind the new body, behind my relationship with Omari, I knew he was right.

In response to my hateful email that I sent him yesterday, Tre told me that I would never be anything more than a desperate side bitch. He told me that his wife's beauty outshined mine beyond anything that my small brain could ever fathom. He said that I was so incompetent of having anything of my own that I wasn't even raising my own baby. He said that I probably only now had my own man because the woman that he really loved was dead.

I sat in the middle of my bed with tears streaming down my face, flowing onto my neck, and falling onto my chest. I was paralyzed with the heart wrenching realization that, even though Tre wasn't even inside of my relationship to know the difference, he was right.

I had gone such lengths to get a man that still had his mind on the love of his life. He was still wrapped up in the thought of her, especially since her likeness lived with us every day, twenty-four seven. I still had little significance. There was nothing tying us together. No love. No history. Just commitment that I borrowed off of his woman's dead body.

I quickly wiped my face when I heard Omari's keys in the door. He often spent some nights at my condo since it was downtown. It felt like he was getting away from the city and the block when he was at my place. Of course, Dahlia was with him. I could hear her cooing as he made his way into the condo.

"Babe?"

"I'm back here."

I quickly left the bed and moved to the mirror to ensure that my face didn't show evidence of my tears. But no matter how much I blotted the dreariness away with press powder and wiped it away with blush and lip-gloss, Omari could see that something wasn't right.

"Hey, baby." I greeted him in the middle of the floor. After setting Dahlia's car seat down on the bed, he hugged me and kissed me softly on the lips.

"What's wrong with you?"

Again, tears began to form in my eyes uncontrollably. No matter how much I wanted to front and act like this was my man that loved me unconditionally, I knew damn well that his love came with an expensive price that I paid just to end up still feeling worthless and insignificant.

"I'm pregnant."

Those words emerged from my lips so effortlessly that it scared me. I feared myself. I feared the lengths that I would go to get rid of this feeling of not being good enough.

I knew that he wouldn't be happy about it. Dahlia was only three months, and he had already told me that we couldn't have kids for some years. But I needed that validity. I needed that importance. I needed that connection with him that gave me the same level of significance as Aeysha and Dahlia.

It was time for me to create that history and life with him that would take away this insecure feeling. I was always a "by any means necessary" kind of bitch, and I was not going to stop until I was Aeysha and Erica.

I only hoped that now that he thought I was pregnant, he would ejaculate into me freely and I would eventually really be pregnant. I saw how he changed when Aeysha got pregnant. I saw how his devotion for family changed how he loved her, and I knew that it would be the same for me.

OMARI

"You're what?"

I'd heard Simone loud and clear, but I just wanted to be sure that this bullshit was really happening.

"I'm pregnant," she told me with sadness. "I know you're upset. I know you don't want any more kids right now, baby. But I'm pregnant. I took a test at work."

This was bad timing; real bad fucking timing. My mind wasn't on other kids right now. Between the block and Dahlia, I had a hard enough time focusing on Simone.

"How many weeks are you?"

"Almost six."

I exhaled as I felt a little relief. There was still time to take care of this.

But, it was as if Simone read the expression in my face. She saw what was coming next and burst into tears.

"You want me to get a fucking abortion?!"

Immediately, I went to her and wrapped my arms around her. She cried into my chest as I attempted to make her feel better. "Baby, that's not what I said."

"That's what you were going to say!"

"It wasn't," I lied. "I wasn't going to say that."

"You're not happy!"

"Of course, I'm not. But you aren't either."

"Because I know you don't want this."

"But it's here. So it is what it is," I said swallowing the lump in my throat.

We stood in the middle of the floor with me holding her tightly. I felt sorry for Simone. I knew that being with me was a lot to handle. Hell, half of the reason why I was lacking on starting a family with her was because my last attempt at starting one left me so heartbroken. I had a guard up; a major one. Just hearing her say that she was pregnant took me to a dark place. I didn't feel the joy that I did when me and Aeysha sat on our bed crying tears of celebration when she told me the same thing. I felt tears, but they were of sorrow that Aeysha never got the chance to see our daughter. They were tears of guilt because I wondered if Aeysha would be mad that I was having another baby already.

I didn't even know how Simone could be pregnant. No, we didn't use condoms. But I pulled out. My babies either got swallowed or died on the sheets.

But there had been so many drunk and sleepy sex sessions that there was no telling.

I giggled, trying to lighten the mood. "Hey. Now

you and Erica can be pregnant together."

I could hear Simone smacking her lips and softly growling as she pulled away from my embrace. I caught her roll her eyes as she moved to the window to wipe her face.

"What's that about?"

Reluctantly, she turned, leaning against the window and looking at me. She folded her arms across her chest. As she stood there with distress all over her face, I couldn't help but admire her body. Fake or not, the shots had done her wonders. That ass was right and so were her hips.

That's probably how I got her knocked up in the first place.

"I heard Tre talking shit while we were there."

"When?"

"When I was on my way to the bathroom. I heard him on the phone with somebody. He was saying how his ghetto ass dope dealing brother-in-law was in his crib and how he needed to get back in the living room before some shit came up missing."

"What?!" That shit pissed me the fuck off. There was no way that Tre should have known my life. Husband or not, Erica shouldn't have felt comfortable telling him no shit like that. "Why would she tell him that I'm hustling?"

Again, Simone rolled her eyes in frustration and came towards me.

I continued to fuss as she put her arms around me. "I don't give a fuck if that's her husband. I don't know that nigga, so he shouldn't know my life. And what the fuck did she tell him to make him think I would take some shit?"

"I don't know," Simone said as she hugged me tight. "But fuck them. You don't need them anyway. Me and Dahlia have been your family way more than they have. Fuck them."

GIA

"Chance, you have to sit up, baby."

I was struggling. It was four in the afternoon and he was still hung over. Rae had been blowing up my phone, trying to come over to get some clothes. But I had to ignore her calls because she would have torn that house up if she knew that Chance was there.

"Urrrgh. I can't move."

"So you're just going to lay here in throw up?"

I was trying to get the pillow cases off of the pillow that he'd just thrown up on after miscalculating the time from the bed to the trash can that I put beside the bed.

"No more drinking for you," I muttered with a giggle as I pushed him over to reveal the pillow underneath him.

"Uhhhh! Please don't do that no more."

I just laughed as I took the pillow case off and held it between two of my acrylic nails. Chance was lucky. Had he not given me such good dick that morning, I would not have been putting up with his drunk stankin' throw up ass.

Damn, that dick was good! Had to be to have me cleaning up a nigga's throw up. I hadn't had dick in years.

And I acted like it. Luckily, he was so drunk that I was sure he wouldn't recall the way I screamed and hollered over that dick all morning. I couldn't help it though. It was so long and thick. He hit spots that I didn't even know I had. And damn did he know how to stroke the pussy. He was damn near dancing in it.

I smiled as the memories crossed my mind while I picked up items of clothing on the floor that he'd managed to throw up on as well.

"I'm going to throw your pants in the wash. I'll be right back, okay?"

Chance merely let out, "Mmm humph."

I laughed and shook my head as I stepped over the rest of our clothes that our drunk asses had stripped off and threw on the ground in anticipation of getting in the bed that morning.

Unexpectedly, Chance's wallet, cell phone, and cash fell out of his pants that I was unknowingly holding upside down as I walked out of the bedroom. As I gathered everything up from the floor to take back into the bedroom, I noticed that his ID said Reginald Barner. Chance's face was on the ID, but that wasn't the name that he told me.

"Chance!" I yelled as I flipped on the light in the room.

"Oh my God. Please turn that light off." His words were muffled into the pillow that he lay face down on.

"Who in the hell is Reginald Barner?! Did you give me a fake name, nigga?!"

That is when Chance rolled over and looked at me. Damn, he looked a hot mess. But that dick was so good that I could easily overlook him drinking too much.

"That's a fake ID," he said nonchalantly.

"And why do you have a fake ID?"

"To get in the club."

My mouth dropped dramatically. "To get in the club?! Oh my God! How old are you?!"

Chance laughed. "Shouldn't you ask that *before* you fuck somebody?"

I was starting to panic. Now that I wasn't drunk, I noticed that, though he was a cutie pie, he looked young. He didn't even have that much facial hair.

"Don't freak out. I'll be nineteen in a few weeks."

"Nineteen?!"

"How old are you?"

"Twenty-three."

"Ooo, a cougar. I like that shit," he moaned seductively as he grabbed a hard dick that was protruding out of his boxers.

Suddenly, I didn't care about his age anymore. If he was a youngin', his dick sure wasn't. That dick was a grown ass man; seasoned meat.

"Whatever, boy. Let me go wash these clothes."

SIX

OMARI

That Saturday was Aeysha's birthday.

I got up early that morning, dressed Dahlia as warm as I could, and took her to see her mother.

She would have turned twenty-six that day. I fought with myself to forget the plans that we made for this birthday right before she died. At first, she wanted a big party since she finally had a job and things were coming together for her. But once she found out that she was pregnant with Dahlia, she wanted the three of us to simply to take a small trip to Wisconsin Dells as a family.

The cemetery was eerie as hell at nine o'clock on a cold winter morning. I fought against the slick, icy, and slushy ground as I held on to Dahlia tightly and walked past grave after grave after grave until we reached Aeysha's headstone. Deflated balloons and dead flowers stuck out from underneath the snow; evidence of my past visits.

I visited Aeysha's grave almost every week.

I came twice a week when I was unable to fake my

way through life and was missing my baby until I had to see some remnants of her again.

This all felt like a crazy dream. One day, she was here. The next, she was gone. In the blink of an eye, with the snap of a finger, she was no longer here as if she was never even here to begin with. If it wasn't for Dahlia, it would be hard to remember her besides my memories, a few pictures, and where she lay at rest.

I stood at her grave; staring at the engraved letters of her name on the headstone and holding Dahlia's cheek against my lips. The smell of Johnson and Johnson overwhelmed me and brought tears to my eyes. There was nothing I loved more than the women that I was in company with. I knew that Aeysha's soul wasn't in that grave, but she definitely lived through Dahlia. They were twins. I was so grateful that God saw fit to give Dahlia her mother's face so that I could see Aeysha in other ways than in my dreams. Dahlia even had her mother's caramel skin, long lashes, and the one lonely dimple in her left cheek.

In a million years, I would have never guessed that, on that day and at that moment, that's where I would be standing. I thought that I had time; time to love Ayesha right, time to show her the man that I could be, time to wife her. That time was taken from me. I blamed myself. I knew that had I been man enough and smart enough to get money legally, Aeysha would be alive. I lived with that guilt every day. Every day I lived in fear that Aeysha's spirit was living on and hating me for putting her in harm's way.

I blamed myself, but I knew that ultimately Ching was at fault. That day, the pain in my heart that stabbed through every vessel every time I thought of the merciless way that nigga shot my love down ached just as bad as it did the day I saw her lifeless body fighting for the ability to live. But on that day, as the small cooing sounds flowing from my beautiful daughter's lips flooded my ears and put the only genuine smile on my face that it's held since her mother died, I knew. I knew then that I was undoubtedly going to kill my cousin.

CHANCE

Life was finally feeling somewhat back to normal. I'd spent the last few days looking for a job. I knew that no job I found would take care of me substantially, but it would be something to hold me down until I figured things out.

I was still living in the motel. Although, on the days I kicked it with Gia, I stayed at her place.

Gia.

Man, just the thought of that girl made me smile like a bitch as I walked through Ford City Mall. I was just walking around the mall wish shopping; wasting time until it was time to hook up with Gia later on that night. That girl definitely made my current situation not so bad. She was a bad ass chick and was a whole lot of fun. We always just laughed, drank, kicked it, and had a good ass time.

Let's not even touch on how good that pussy was.

Jesus!

That pussy was tight as air; like she hadn't had dick in years. She responded to the dick in the same manner; like it was new to her. I don't know if she just had some good pussy or if older pussy just knew how to fuck better. Either way, I was sold. If I could fuck with shorty and sleep

in a house that smelled like Febreze, rather than a stankin'
ass motel, I was more than good with that.

"Yo', Chance!"

I was caught off guard when I heard my name as I
stood staring into the window of Foot Locker at the new
Jordans. They were damn near three hundred dollars so
they would never touch my feet, but it didn't hurt to look.

"Aw, man! What's up, my dude?" When I turned to
see who was calling me, I recognized Capone. Instantly, I
wondered what in the hell he was doing on this side of
town. I knew him from out west. We went to high school
together. Eventually he dropped out of high school because
he was getting money on the streets.

As we shook up, I asked him, "What *you* doin' out
here?"

"Naw, man. What you doin' out here?"

We were both raised out west. It was rare to see
Westside niggas on the Southside; especially Capone. He
got money all day on a block near Lexington House. I
walked by him slangin' on a daily basis. I would even ask
him to put me on. He always refused though. Even though
we were around the same age, he would always tell me that
I needed to just stay in school so that I could get out of
Lexington and make a better life for myself.

"I moved out here a few weeks ago," was the condensed version that I told him.

"What happened to you? I heard on the streets that you had just up and disappeared."

Automatically, my heart started skipping beats, but I knew Capone couldn't possibly know anything about Aeysha. It was the guilt that automatically made my blood pressure rise just because he referenced how I up and left town.

"I went to Minnesota. Tried to get on."

"Tried?"

"Yea. I got robbed, to be honest," I told him with an embarrassing laugh.

Laughing along with me, Capone said, "That's fucked up, joe."

Capone motioned for me to follow him inside of Foot Locker. As I did, we kept rapping; catching up on niggas we use to hang with and bitches we use to fuck with out west. He tried on so many pair of shoes that I got tired of watching. First thing he did was cop them new Jays, on top of about five other joints.

I was jealous as hell.

"Aye, man. You still servin'?"

As Capone and I walked out of the Foot Locker, he

held a slick grin on his face. I knew he was selling drugs. No way was he working a nine to five, and no way was he able to drop over a grand on gym shoes on a whim unless he was about to get that grand right back in fast money.

"Something like that," was his answer.

"You got some work for me?"

He looked cautious. He looked at nothing in particular as we slowed our pace outside of the Foot Locker. "Honestly, I could use some more manpower that I trust. Me and my nigga thinking about setting up shop on a new block in the burbs."

Now, my heart was racing in anticipation. My mouth started to water with greed. Capone saw the happiness in my face that I didn't even try to hide and laughed.

He still looked reluctant though, so I started to practically beg for a chance to get put on. "C'mon, Capone, man. I need to get this money. Don't play me like we still in high school. I'm grown and I need some grown money."

"You sure you wanna be 'bout this life?"

"Real talk, it's not a question. I'm out of options."

Some niggas sold drugs because it was easy. I honestly would have taken a different route, but drug money was faster than legal money. I needed fast money before my ass didn't even have the nasty ass motel to sleep in.

"A'ight, man. I'mma fuck with you because I know you. Take my number and holla at me in a few days."

"Tiana, I need you to watch Dahlia for a minute."

Tiana looked at me like I was crazy. I had just walked into the spot out south. I knew that she could see that something was going on. I would never have my baby in the spot. But it was an emergency.

"I'll be right back," I tried to convince her.

"You sure?"

"I swear. C'mon."

"A'ight, Omari. Come right back. I got plans."

Every time I left Aeysha's grave, I left with a bigger scar on my heart. But that day the scar was massive and burned like salt in a fresh wound.

I dropped Dahlia off to Tiana, jumped back in my ride, and bent blocks at record speeds. I wasn't even thinking. I just felt rage and was heavily seeking revenge. Visions of the digits of Aeysha's blood pressure rapidly lowering fueled my rage as I swerved through lanes on Seventy-First Street.

When I got to Ching's block, I pulled over at the corner and turned off my headlights. Never did I think to stop. I reached into my glove compartment for the .38 that I kept inside. It was about seven o'clock in the evening. The sun had just set. Just a few people were on the streets. I put the car in drive and crept up the street slowly until I was in front of Ching's crib.

My mind was still pregnant with thoughts of Aeysha. Visions of me attempting to tell my baby girl that her mother was dead, whenever she could comprehend death, made me sick to my stomach. I wiped the tears away that flowed from my bloodshot eyes as I rolled down the window and pointed the gun at Ching's house. I thought of Aeysha and I fired repeatedly. Bullets whizzed through the cold biting winter air like parachute fireworks.

The few pedestrians on the block could be heard screaming as bullets pierced the windows of Ching's house. Bullets shot through the front door and pierced the siding of the house.

I shot until my finger hurt. I shot until there were no bullets and I was firing out air.

Then I sped off.

Flying down Aberdeen at record speeds, I realized how good that felt. I'd released three months of pent up vengeful frustrations. For five minutes, I felt better. But as the minutes and seconds slipped by as I flew east on Seventy-Ninth Street towards the e-way, I knew that that wasn't enough. That wasn't enough for Ching to pay for what he'd done to Aeysha.

But it was a start.

It was a warning.

My cell phone started to ring as it lay in my lap. I wasn't in the mood to talk to no motherfuckin' body, but when I saw that it was Capone, I answered.

"Whad up?"

"Did you just shoot up Ching's crib?"

I glanced at the clock with a smile. It had only been fifteen minutes since I left Ching's block. I was damn near back in Riverdale.

"Did he get hit?"

"Hell naw."

Instantly, regret filled my heart. I knew that I was just aiming randomly, but I was just hoping that I'd hit that nigga.

A warning was good enough though. I wasn't quite ready to kill him. I wanted to fuck with him for a little while first.

"He wasn't there. His girl was there though."

A small evil grin ran across my face as I thought of that ratchet bitch running through the house, scared and taking cover.

"You did that shit, homey?" Capone had a slight laugh in his words as he questioned me. "We were supposed to do this shit together."

"I ain't done nothing yet. How you find out so fast?"

"She called him. He was at the spot out west. Word spreads, man. Nobody has ever shot at Ching."

"Well, somebody is about to start."

GIA

"Just ignore it."

Chance convinced me to ignore my cell phone as he punished me doggy style on the side of the bed. My bare French manicured feet were planted on the carpet. My face was buried amongst the sheet. Chance stood tall behind me slowly and deeply penetrating my pussy with long and deep strokes.

"Sssss." I hissed and moaned to withstand the stress the size of his dick put on my pussy. It hurt so good.

I couldn't believe that this little boy was fucking me like this.

"Right there, baby." I spoke breathlessly with lustful pleas. "Please, don't stop. Right there."

Chance had the same lust in his giggles as his strokes got right where I wanted them and stayed there, rhythmically hitting that spot over and over again with persistence.

"Oh God! Oh fuck!" I was gritting my teeth as I forced myself to withstand that dick. Chance held onto my waist and gave me the business. I was delusional with satisfaction and lust. But I wasn't so delusional that I didn't hear noises at the doorway of my bedroom.

Curiously, I glanced in that direction.

When I saw her reflection, I jumped out of my skin.
"Rae!"

In reaction to my fear, Chance jumped. We were tangled amongst each other as I fought to find something to cover myself. The light was on in my bedroom, so we all saw each other clear as day. Chance seemed scared at first. Then, it's as if he figured out that Rae was really a woman, and lost any fear. Chance hurriedly threw on his pants. I threw myself into a shirt. Unfortunately, it was Chance's, so that only hurt Rae even more.

"What the fuck are you doing here?!" I was so pissed! I couldn't believe the size balls this bitch had. "How long have you been standing there?!"

Rae just stared at me, looking as if she'd just swallowed her own shit. She was disgusted, mortified, and evidently hurt as tears streamed down her face. Chance looked back and forth between us curiously. His eyes asked me so many questions while being obviously amused at the lady-boy that stood in the doorway.

"Chance, can you give me a minute?"

Rae's chest heaved. "Give you a minute?! Fuck you mean, give you a minute?! Make this nigga leave!"

My arms flailed as I yelled at the top of my lungs. "You can't tell me what to do! WE ARE NOT TOGETHER!"

Rae and Chance stared one another down as Chance walked out of the room.

Coolly, Chance glided by Rae, looking her up and down like she was a peon. Then he told me, "I'll be in the living room, baby," just to fuck with her some more.

Rae bit her lip. She was biting it so hard that her teeth were making impressions in the pinkness of her lip. She closed the door and immediately came to me. As she held my arms, all of the aggression and anger that she had just held was now submissive, passive, and humble.

"Baby, please don't leave me. Not like this. Not for this nigga."

"I am not leaving you for him, Rae," I told her as I escaped from her embrace. "I am leaving you because I have had enough. I don't want to be with you anymore."

Rae was heartbroken. Her tears flowed like a sad waterfall. I felt sorry for her, but I felt sorrier for the unhappy girl that I was when I was with her. This past month had been such a freeing and enjoyable experience that I was not willing to let go for the captive and insecure relationship that she was offering.

"Do you love this nigga?"

"Rae…"

"I'll share you, baby. I'll share you with him," she begged as she reached for me again. I sat on the bed, on the very spot that Chance was just wearing me out in. I longed to be back in that moment, with his dick in me, rather than looking into the pitiful eyes of a lost soul.

"Are you serious, Rae? Listen to yourself."

Like a sad puppy, she stood there crying. I knew her heart was broken, but it was something that I couldn't fix. Rae needed help. She needed therapy and to find herself an identity that she wasn't ashamed to show the world.

We stared each other down for a few moments. I believe that she wanted me to find some sympathy for her tears, but there was none in me. I had lust for the dick waiting on me in the living room; lust that didn't have time to argue with this bitch.

"So that's it?"

I sighed heavily and ran my fingers through my weave. My hair was still damp from the pounding I was taking from Chance that drenched me with sweat. "I told you. I can't do this."

Quietly, Rae simply stood. Naturally I flinched as she walked by me, remembering the last time we were in

102

such close contact. Yet, she continued to walk by as she wiped her face free of her sorrow. She opened the door and walked out without a word. Even though she didn't hit me, I was still in fear. I didn't want to be with her, but I still loved her enough to fear what leaving her would do to her.

SEVEN

OMARI

"So what you think about my guy?"

I didn't really think much about Chance, one of Capone's guys that he wanted to put on the block. I hadn't met him yet, but Capone had been telling me how he wanted to do him a favor and put him to work.

"It ain't about what I think," I told Capone, glancing at him in the passenger seat. "He's your guy. If you fucks with him, then I fucks with him. Long as he can move that product, I'm good with him."

"I'm sure he can. He from the hood. Won't be hard to teach him if it ain't in him already."

"Is that a jab, nigga?"

Capone chuckled as he lit his blunt. "Hell yea."

"Whatever."

He was right though. I'd gone from a broke pretty boy to a street nigga with ease. Contrary to Capone thinking it had to do with him educating me on the game, this cold exterior that was turning me into this calculating savage day by day had more so to do with the anger I felt behind Ayesha's death.

"You sure you don't want to get one of them young niggas to do this?"

I chuckled. "You?"

"Whatever, man. You know what I mean. The young boys amped up and ready for some shit like this. We ain't gotta get our hands dirty. We can grab one of them trigger happy motherfuckers that don't give a fuck."

Again, I chuckled, now with a bit of sarcasm. "I don't give a fuck. I'll be trigger happy in one minute."

"A'ight, boss. I got your back. Just making sure."

Truth be told, I was tired of innocent bloodshed. Aeysha's blood was more than enough. If it wasn't Ching, Smoke, Burt, or Black, I didn't want anybody dying on account of this war. Besides, I wanted my hands on every bit of this fight because it was my fight. I was going to make Ching's life a living fucking hell. I wanted to be right there, front and center, when the bodies dropped.

I thought I would have second thoughts. The move that Capone and I were about to pull was going to be the start of a war that would last until either Ching or I was in the ground. He wasn't the type of man that let anybody get away with fucking with his money. I saw it firsthand. But I had become the same type of nigga not to be fucked with.

When we pulled up in front of one of Ching's traps that once housed Capone, I felt no reluctance. I was convinced that this shit I was about to kick off was destiny.

With hoods over our faces and guns gripped in our pockets, we walked up to the door. At five in the morning, the streets were so quiet that you could hear the snow falling and the wind whipping through the gangways and alleys.

However, gunshots soon pierced the silence. We shot our way through the front door of the old brick house. As expected, a block boy was sleep on the couch, the only furniture in the front room. He darted under the couch where Capone told me the artillery was kept. But I was on top of it. Before he could get his hand on his strap, I was standing on top of his arm; breaking it as I put more and more weight on it.

"Aaaargh!" He had to be only sixteen years old. He was small, frail and short. "Aw, shit! My arm!"

Capone had quickly moved to the back of the house where he knew the weight was stashed. Since he used to hustle out of this spot, he knew the ins and outs of every stash spot. We didn't even have to cop more weight to set up shop in Riverdale. I was setting up shop with Ching's shit. Thanks to the connect talking way too much with a drunk tongue, I knew that Ching had just copped weight.

This was a win/win.

The dude under my feet was frantically screeching and squirming. I didn't say a word. I simply pointed the gun at his head and stared into his eyes, daring him to make a move as I heard bones breaking under my Timberland boots.

Not even three minutes later, Capone was coming back into the living room carrying two large dusty garbage bags.

"Let's move," was all he said as he walked towards the front door that hung off the hinges and let in the winter cold.

Pow! *Pow*!

I let off two shots into the dude's leg to keep him from chasing us to the car with gunfire. I was also keeping Ching from killing him. He couldn't have explained letting us get away all this weight without even a scratch on him. He still had one arm to shoot with. I knew Ching well enough to know that he would want to know why he hadn't used it.

Those slugs in his leg were keeping him alive.

SIMONE

A few weeks after telling Omari that I was pregnant, he was finally settled into the idea that I was having a baby.

Just like I thought, now that I was "pregnant", he was freely cumming in me every chance he got. Yet, as I sat on the toilet in the bathroom of my master bedroom, I grimaced at the sight of blood.

I wasn't pregnant.

And now I would have to spend days hiding the fact that I was on my period.

Something had to be done quickly. Finally, Omari was warming up to me more. I was not only his girlfriend. I was his baby's mother, and he was treating me as such. He was the family man that I knew he would be as soon as we became one.

"Miss Simone, I'm about to go! I'm leaving Dahlia on your bed. She's asleep."

From inside of the bathroom, I told Tiana, "Okay, thank you! See you later."

I sat on the toilet while looking into the mirror at myself wondering what the fuck I had gotten myself into. I needed to get pregnant. I had to have a baby. Finally Omari was showing some happiness about this pregnancy and I was starting to feel secure in this relationship.

I had to think of something.

Dahlia's cries broke me out of my train of thought. I rolled my eyes into the back of my head and just continued to sit there, now with my head in my hands. I was wracking my brain trying to figure out why I wasn't pregnant yet. I'd done the calculations. I was sure to have sex while I was ovulating.

Mother Nature was not on my side.

Again, Dahlia's cries pierced through the air. I longed for the moment that Omari got there. Continuously, she screamed like a maniac. So I stopped my brainstorming, put in a tampon, and stormed out of the bathroom.

"Shut up already," I groaned walking towards the bed where Dahlia lay crying and kicking her little legs.

Without even thinking, I muffed her. Though it was only a slight nudge, her cries became high-pitched and I saw a small cut on her lip that leaked blood. I noticed the ring on my hand and realized that I had nicked her lip with it.

"Shit!"

I raced to get a tissue to wipe the blood. Omari was going to be there at any moment.

Just as I expected, as soon as I was back inside of the bedroom cleaning Dahlia's lip, I heard Omari's keys in the front door of my condo. I scooped Dahlia into my arms and began to rock her. I tried to calm her down by giving her the pacifier, but she wasn't soothed. She continued to whine, and my skin crawled.

"What's wrong with Daddy's baby?"

My eyes rolled as I could hear Omari coming down the hall. He appeared inside of the bedroom door, looking beautiful and full of swag as always. He'd just gotten his locs styled into long braids that went down his back.

He didn't kiss me. He didn't say hello to me. Nor did he even hug me. He immediately came into the room and took Dahlia out of my arms.

I was still in competition with the next bitch.

OMARI

"What the fuck is wrong with her lip?"

I sat on Simone's bed glaring at, what looked like, a fresh cut on my daughter's lip.

As Simone fixed her hair in the mirror that hung on her wall, she nonchalantly replied, "I was just looking at that. I saw it after Tiana dropped her off."

"I'm beating her ass." Before I knew it, I grabbed my cell out of my pocket while holding Dahlia in my other hand.

Simone spun around. "Who?!"

"Tiana."

"Omari, put the phone down! That girl did not do that to her."

"Well, why the fuck she always got bruises and shit on her?! It's not like she can walk, so she can't be walking around falling into shit. What the fuck, man?!"

"Omari, calm down." Simone was now sitting next to me. She lay her hand on my thigh and started to rub it to soothe me. "Tiana is not abusing Dahlia. You're tripping."

"Well, she isn't watching her carefully."

"She is a baby. It was probably a toy."

I took a deep breath and tried to calm down. Dahlia was everything to me, and I could admit that I was over protective when it came to every inch of her skin and every hair on her head.

"Anyway. Look. I need to talk to you about the move."

Capone and I noticed the drought out in Riverdale. There were minimal blocks with supply but a whole lot of demand. After robbing Ching, Capone and I had the necessary weight to set up shop in my crib in Riverdale.

So, me and Dahlia had to move in with Simone.

"When are you coming?"

"In about a week." Just then, Dahlia began to gurgle, coo, and flash big smiles at me. I smiled along with her as I asked Simone, "You ready for me and Dahlia to move into your space?"

Simone smiled and kissed Dahlia on the cheek, "Of course I am."

"You think you're going to be able to handle two small kids?"

Suddenly, my smile was gone and Simone saw that. I was speaking real shit to her that I wanted her to listen to. I wasn't ready for another baby. I was going to support her anyway she went, but she needed to realize what she was getting into all for the sake of having my baby.

"It will be a bit much to handle, but I can do it."

"Are you sure?"

I wanted her to understand me, to realize what she was getting into. She had me. I was there. Her need to constantly plant her seed was unnecessary. She was always trying to push things to the next level as if she didn't have me where she wanted me. I knew that since I put Aeysha before her, she always had this insecurity when it came to me and this relationship. I didn't want her to allow insecurity to push her to have a baby that we weren't ready for.

She saw my reluctance and got angry. "Why do you keep asking me that?"

"Because there is still time…"

"Time for what?!"

At the sound of her booming voice, Dahlia jumped. I instantly held her to my chest and

Simone rolled her eyes.

"So you're choosing Dahlia over my baby?!"

"I didn't say that and stop yelling."

She bit down on her lip and rolled her eyes into the back of her head. While she was calming her nerves, I took the opportunity to make my point. "All I'm saying is that I want you to realize that when you have this baby you will be raising a one year old and an infant. I won't be here that much. I gotta get this money."

"I got this," was her reply as she smiled. It was a sarcastic and evil smile. "Don't worry about me. I always take care of myself."

CHANCE

"Bitch."

I groaned under my breath as I rode the Red Line to Ninety-Fifth Street. From there, I would take the bus to Riverdale to meet up with Capone at the new spot.

The possibility of getting money should have had me in a happier place, but it had been nearly a month since the last time I'd seen or talked to Simone. Though she promised that she would take care of things, she was ghost, just like I thought. She wasn't answering my text messages, and she was straight sending me to voicemail when I called.

I still had a few dollars, but just in case things didn't work out with Capone, I needed her to do something. I was in this predicament because of her. I could have been in transitional housing living scott-free for three more years. They would have even helped me find a job.

I liked fucking Gia, but I especially fucked her to keep a warm roof over my head and hot meals. But no woman wants a guy laying up in her house sucking in her heat and watching her cable without contributing. Luckily, Gia was a down chick that knew my struggles, so she wasn't judging me. She was just having fun and enjoying the dick.

Because of this conniving bitch, Simone, I was homeless and broke while she rode clean and ate good. That shit was really starting to piss me off. Even though for months I'd figured that Simone played me, the fact that I'd murdered someone for this bitch and she didn't even think enough of me to answer the fucking phone was really starting to fuck with me.

During the rest of the train and bus rides, I blew up Simone's cell a couple more times. I started to wonder who I killed. I wondered if she was a nice girl; as innocent as I was in Simone's ploys. But I had to make myself stop thinking about it because it was literally making me sick with headache and a messed up stomach.

I tried to push those thoughts to the back of my mind as I reached the block that the new trap house was on in Riverdale on 147th and Peoria.

Just like Capone said, his partner's red Challenger was sitting outside. That motherfucker looked nice. On the phone, Capone told me how he and his boy basically started from nothing and now had two blocks. I only hoped that I could have such luck. But, in the mean time, pocketing three hundred dollars off of every quarter I put in the streets during my shift was good enough for now. I was so hungry for bread that I was willing to do whatever it took to sell water to a fish, so I could easily push one or two quarters a day if the drought in this area was as serious as Capone claimed.

Still in all, no matter the possibility of money that was approaching and no matter the possibility of pussy that was waiting on me when I got to Gia's later on that night, thoughts of Simone were still consuming me. I couldn't shake this eerie feeling that was over me because of her.

I felt stupid.

I felt played.

After ringing the doorbell, a tall dude with locs opened the door. Instantly, I assumed that he was some pretty boy. I had never seen a black person with gray eyes. Instantly, I assumed that I was at the wrong crib.

That is, until he said, "Whad up? You Chance?"

"Yea," I answered cautiously.

"I'm Omari, bro. C'mon on in."

As I followed him into the house, I realized that this was the dude Capone was telling me about; his partner. I looked around the house and was real suspect. It definitely didn't look like a trap house. As a matter of fact, it was nice as hell and looked like a family was staying there.

I even peeped a baby's room.

Something was eerily familiar about the air in that house. It was the smell. For some reason, the smell in that house put me in the mind of something familiar. But at the time, I had too much shit on my mind to really try to put my finger on it. What I needed to focus on was this money. I pushed everything to the back of my mind, even Simone, and sat at the kitchen table with Omari where Capone was rolling a blunt and telling me the ins and outs of this new operation that would make them richer and me less poor.

GIA

After almost a month of fucking with Chance, I had feelings towards him that I hadn't had towards a man since I was in high school.

As he lay on top of me giving me the best missionary ever, that's exactly how I felt; like I was back in high school. I had butterflies in my stomach when I thought about his sexy ass during the day. I reread our text message conversations like a lame.

I had a soft spot in my heart for men that I never had before. I wasn't in love or anything, but I was definitely in lust. I liked him. We kicked it well together. I trusted him, when I had never trusted a man in my life. We were real with each other. He was so open with who he was. Any other guy would have lied about being broke, homeless, and carless. His honesty made me feel like I can trust him and trust him with me.

"Argh! Shit!" Chance began to let out deep moans as his rhythm became faster and more consistent.

He was cumming.

I encouraged him. "C'mon on, baby."

"Oh shit."

"That's it, baby."

"Aaaaaargh!" Chance squeezed my waist and put all of his body weight on me as he enjoyed his release. I rubbed his back, my hands drenched in his sweat, as he cursed under his short and heavy breaths.

"Damn, girl," he said as he rolled over on his back. His dick was now only semi-erect with his nut dangling at the tip of the Magnum.

Through heavy breaths of my own, I asked, "You put the chain on the door?"

He burst out laughing, and even I had to giggle.

"Hell, I wanna know. I'm serious."

"Why? Scared your *boyfriend* is going to come back?"

Again, I was laughing, "Whatever, Chance."

"You almost got me beat up," he said poking his lip out.

"Yea right."

After Rae left that night, I had a lot of explaining to do. Though Chance and I had been real with each other, I had never explained to him that the ex, that I spoke of so frequently, was a woman. He admitted that he noticed the pictures in my bedroom and was just waiting on me to explain.

Even when I thought that stunt Rae pulled would have scared him away, it hadn't. He laughed his ass off. He thought it was hilarious that this woman was head over heels for me. He couldn't fathom the idea of two people of the same sex having such issues. I laughed it off as well, because I knew it would be hard for him to understand.

Eventually, Chance got out of the bed and went towards the wastebasket. As he removed the condom, he told me, "Yea, I put the chain on, scary ass."

"Whatever."

As Chance climbed back into bed and lay next to me, he suddenly got serious.

"Look. I won't be around as much anymore."

"Why? You got a wife you never told me about?"

He kissed my cheek as he spooned with me. "Hell naw. You're my wife."

Surprisingly, that didn't make me flinch. My insides curled up into a girlish smile, and I laughed at the butterflies that flew around in my stomach.

"But real talk though. I hooked up with one of my dudes from high school. He wants me to serve out of one of his spots. It's a new spot, so I'll be putting in a lot of work. But you got me during any free time I have."

Though he was using a lot of street talk to explain

himself, I knew that that meant he was serving. I had no issues with that because, shit, I was a stripper. I knew the pains of having to get down how you lived to make some money. But I wasn't ready to deal with the petty issues that came with fucking with a man, so I definitely wasn't ready to deal with the major issues that came with fucking with a nigga in the dope game.

Yet, the possibilities of having a man with drug money sounded beautiful to my closet.

Drug money; a gift and a curse.

EIGHT

CHANCE

I had been serving for two weeks. It was a new spot, so product moved slowly at first. But Capone and Omari were right about it being a drought. Once the fiends smelled the heroine in the air and the party boys tasted the loud and molly, the block was jumping.

I was posted on the block like a mailbox. I didn't care how cold it was; I stood outside all day and at all hours of the night serving every crack head, every street nigga, and every white boy. Capone bounced between the spots collecting money and watching the bitch in the kitchen cutting down bricks like a scientist. She was some white hype by the name of Paula that stayed cooking in that kitchen as long as she was able to cuff an eight ball of heroin in exchange for the work every night.

I barely saw Omari. He stayed low key. He was a private dude. When I would ask Capone about him, Capone was always mum's the word. He only said that, after a situation a few months ago, Omari was hush-hush about the details of his personal life. Only certain people were privy to that information; basically, only Capone.

That was cool with me. I didn't have to know anything about Omari. We didn't have to be cool, and we didn't have to be friends; as long as he let me get this money.

Finally the motel was no longer my home. If I wasn't at the spot, I was at Gia's crib fucking her brains out.

After serving two crack heads a couple bags of heroin, I checked my cell for the umpth-teenth time. Every time I checked it and saw that Simone still saw fit to ignore my calls and text messages, I got madder and madder. Despite the twenty-five degree day, my face was hot with rage at the audacity of this bitch. For all she knew, I was living on the streets with not a dollar to my name, and she didn't even care enough to call and even act like she gave a fuck.

I was just calling her at this point to prove a point. I forced back that appalling feeling that being played gave me and kept working. Luckily, I didn't even need that bitch anymore. The way that I was hustling, I was pocketing four to five hundred dollars a day. That weekend, I was copping a used whip. Capone knew a guy selling a 2001 Chevy for two grand. It probably would barely make it to Riverdale, but it was better than that cold ass bus.

All in all, things were finally looking up.

SIMONE

Erica's name continuously flashed on Omari's cell phone while he was in the shower. My first thought was to answer, but it was better to just ignore her call.

Then, I erased the call from the call log all together. Fuck that bitch.

After I told Omari what I heard Tre saying at their house that day, he wasn't fucking with them anymore. That is exactly what I wanted when I told him that lie. Fuck Tre. I'll be damned if I have to sit around him and that bitch amongst their happily ever after with him looking down on me.

I continued getting dressed for dinner. I stood before the full length mirror staring at my new hips and ass as I slipped on a pair of leggings that would look great with the knee high boots that I had just bought from Nordstrom's. I hated to have to ruin such a perfect body with a baby, but I had to do what I had to do. Fortunately, I had another four or five months before I actually was supposed to look pregnant.

"What you got a taste for, babe?"

Omari caught me off guard as he walked into the

bedroom wearing nothing but droplets of water and a towel.

Gawd damn, he was fine. It was amazing how he still managed to stay in the gym while building business with Capone. He was most of the reason why I was also in shape. We often went to the gym together.

I naturally gravitated towards him. I took the bottle of Vaseline Gel from the dresser as I walked by. Once in front of Omari, I gently pushed him down on the bed. He smiled bashfully as I laid him down on his stomach and removed the towel.

I dried his body submissively. Then I took the Vaseline Gel and began to moisturize his skin,

"I'm craving pizza," I finally answered. "I've been craving pizza like crazy."

I wanted him to smile and say something sweet about our baby, but he didn't. I shook off the regret and continued to rub the oil into his gorgeous dark skin while wondering if this beautiful specimen of man had any idea the lengths I took and was willing to take just to wake up next to him every day.

Dahlia's cries broke the love that my hands were making to Omari's body. Without hesitation, he moved so fast that he nearly knocked me off of the bed. He left out of the room like lightning.

When I once thought it was never possible to be jealous of someone that couldn't even wipe their own ass, I was jealous of Dahlia. He was obsessed with that damn girl in the way that I wished he would obsess after me.

Twenty minutes later, Omari and I were fully dressed and waiting for Tiana so that we could go to dinner. At first, Omari insisted that we bring Dahlia. I convinced him that a loud restaurant was not a good place for a four month old. So, just as I thought he would, he called Tiana over to watch her for a couple of hours.

"Why don't you wait for Tiana and then meet me at Beggars? I can stop at the spot real quick in the meantime."

Like a good little girl, I said okay and waited for Tiana who arrived no more than five minutes after Omari pulled off.

"I'm so sorry," Tiana apologized as she came through the door looking cute and smelling good.

"Going somewhere?" I looked her up and down with a fake smile as we stood at the front door. My Michael Kors bag was hanging on my arm and my keys were in my hand.

"No," she answered. She tried to appear innocent but I saw right through that shit.

"Yea okay," I said short and dry.

"Is Dahlia sleep?"

"Yea," I groaned. "For now. But you know her crying ass gone wake up any second now."

Tiana walked into the house shaking her head and laughing. "You been so mean since you got knocked up. Is that pregnancy hormones?"

I lingered by the front door until Tiana disappeared into the living room.

"Whatever," I said with a fake laugh as I peeked down the hall to ensure that she had disappeared into the living room.

Before leaving out of the house, I double checked the patio door and ADT system.

"I'm gone, Tiana!"

"Bye, Ms. Simone!"

OMARI

My eyes were glued on the playoff games while I stuffed my face with sausage and pepperoni pizza. In my right hand was a Corona that helped wash it down. Simone sat beside me with her hand on my thigh talking my ear off about baby this and baby that.

I heard her ask, "What do you think we should name it if it's a girl?"

She didn't understand that a conversation like this was hella hard for me. I had just had these conversations with the love of my life a few months ago, and now she was dead. This shit was uncomfortable for me while it was heaven on earth for Simone.

But I tried to be supportive anyway, while my eyes stayed glued on the game. "I don't know, baby. What you think?"

She rambled off names into my ear, but the sounds of jump shots, whistles being blown and my thoughts drowned her out. I was thinking about Ching and wondering when he would put two and two together that it was me and Capone hitting up his spots. We'd just hit another one that morning. Surprisingly, it was empty without a block boy on post. We stuck that nigga for three hundred thousand dollars worth of coke, pills, and mollies in street money. It was easier stealing from Ching than coping from the connect. Both of my spots were cracking, and my stash spots were over flowing with extra cash.

"Now, if it's a boy, I want to name him after his daddy," I heard Simone say before she kissed me on the cheek.

I smiled and nodded.

"Gawd damn right," I said with my eyes still on Dwayne Wade. Out of my peripheral, I saw Simone's iPhone light up as if it were ringing but the ringer was on silent. She looked at the phone and put it down as she tried to hide some irritation. She had been doing that a lot lately; ignoring calls and leaving her ringer on silent.

But my phone rang before I could bring that up. It was Tiana, so I answered, despite missing a layup by Lebron that was going to tie the game if it went in. "What's up, Ti…"

"Omari, you gotta come home!"

I heard the terror in her voice. There was a sense of panic in her voice that was all too familiar.

I jumped up recognizing the horror.

"What's wrong?!"

I couldn't hear Tiana over her tears and Simone's constant questions. "Omari, what's wrong?! Where are you going?!"

I was already walking away from the table though. I was on my way out of Beggars as I heard Tiana say, "Dahlia isn't breathing! I came in to check on her and she wasn't breathing! Oh my God!"

"Did you call 9-1-1?!"

"Yes! I hear them coming down the block now! Hurry up, please!"

I ran to my car, not even checking to see if Simone was behind me. Luckily, when I was opening the driver's side door, Simone was almost at the car also. She was looking at me like I was crazy and confused.

"Dahlia isn't breathing," was all I could say as I hopped in the car. I sped off before Simone could even close the door, leaving her car behind.

OMARI

Twenty minutes.

I drove ninety miles an hour, running red lights and taking shortcuts, but it still took me twenty minutes to get from Harvey to Simone's condo.

Twenty minutes.

Twenty minutes was all it took for the paramedics to get there, attempt to resuscitate Dahlia, and pronounce her dead. As I ran up to the building, I spotted police officers and cars. The eerily familiar scene made my heart pound and my head spin. I tried to hold it together as I ran inside of the building. Neighbors stood in the hallways trying to see what was going on. The front door of Simone's condo was wide open. Paramedics, police officers, and detectives were standing around the kitchen. Tiana sat at the table with tears streaming down her face as some nigga stood behind her with his hand on her back and in his socks and wife beater, as if he'd been in this motherfucker comfortably for quite some time.

Tiana's signature huge lashes were gone. Her makeup looked clownish as it smeared all over her eyes.

"Where is she?"

Tiana looked scared to even answer me. When our eyes met, she buried her face in her hands and started to bawl uncontrollably. A female officer standing behind her comforted her as another officer led me and Simone into the baby's room.

And there she was. There was my angel lying there so peacefully and beautifully. She looked asleep. She looked alive and like, if I touched her, she would react to Daddy's touch like she always did. But she didn't. I touched her. When I felt the change in her skin, the coldness of it, I lost it.

Simone threw her arms around me, and I buried my face into her shoulder.

"It was more than likely SIDS," I heard someone say.

I couldn't even react. I was paralyzed with pain. Besides being my baby, Dahlia was all of Aeysha that I had left.

"Son, son..." I could hear the officer calling me, trying to calm me down so that he could talk to me. "I just have a few questions, and then we can get out of your hair and let you grieve."

"Omari, come on, baby. You need to answer his questions. You can do this."

Just like when Aeysha passed, Simone was there for me; holding my hand and wiping my tears, even though she had tears of her own.

I saw the body bag that one of the paramedics tried to hide behind her back. It was so little and tiny. Just the sight of it ignited the pain in my heart all over again. She looked at the anguish in my eyes and her heart went out to me.

They let me say my goodbyes before I left the room to talk to the officer. They let me pick her up and hold her. I sat in the rocking chair near the window and held her, kissing her cold face over and over again, until they had to pry her out of my arms.

As I handed her to the paramedic, Simone gave her a quick kiss as well.

Then Simone and I followed the officer out of the room. I noticed that the paramedics closed the door behind us. I tried talking myself off of the edge of the cliff. I told myself not to jump. I tried hard not to go back to that dark place where I was after Aeysha was killed, a dark place that I had only managed to escape from just a little bit, a dark place that I went back to visit every now and then.

I held Simone's hand and barely listened to the police officer.

"I couldn't help but notice some bruises on Dahlia. Though it's most likely SIDS, we're going to do an autopsy to verify that." Then the officer lowered his voice, "Do you think anyone was abusing Dahlia? The babysitter? Her boyfriend? Is he around the baby often?"

My heart was racing. Anxiety set in and magnified into fury. I couldn't speak as vomit threatened to make an appearance.

I just stared into nothing as Simone answered for me, "I always assumed that she had a boy in the house while she was babysitting."

"And the bruises?"

"I've seen the bruises. Omari noticed them too," Simone told the officer. "But I never thought Tiana would do such a thing."

"Figure it out and press charges against that bitch," I spit.

The officer and Simone looked at me alarmingly.

"Tiana is like family to you," Simone told me. "Officer, accidents happen, and I am sure that's all those bruises were." Then she looked at me again. "Babe, you can't be serious."

"Figure it out," I told the officer. "Do what you gotta do."

NINE

OMARI

Ironically, two days after Dahlia passed I pulled up in front of the spot on Riverdale and saw Eboni standing in the yard talking to Capone.

No matter the bullshit she was on right before Aeysha got killed, admittedly it was good to see her. Her presence reminded me of Aeysha, of good times and a place in time that I would have loved to go back to. I had to hide my happiness to see Eboni since Simone was with me. We were at the spot to get some more of my things to take back to her place.

"Oh, there he go right there," I heard Capone tell her as me and Simone hopped out of the car.

Both Eboni and I attempted to look at each other nonchalantly because we could feel Simone looking on curiously.

I introduced them to each other while praying for no jealous beef from either one of them. "Simone, this is Eboni, my old neighbor. She was Aeysha's friend."

"Hi," Simone told her quickly as she barely waved. "Nice to meet you."

Eboni looked at her curiously. I knew that she probably felt some type of way because I was with another woman so soon after Aeysha's death.

"I'm going in the house, babe. It's cold," Simone told me. Before she could say anything else, before I could respond, she quickly walked off and was heading into the house.

"I'll give y'all some privacy," Capone told me as he followed Simone.

Eboni continued to look suspiciously as Capone walked towards the crib. I just knew that she was about to give me an earful about having a new woman, but frankly I didn't owe Eboni shit. She hadn't been the most loyal friend to Aeysha, so she wasn't really in the position to say shit.

But as soon as the front door closed, Eboni told me, "I know her."

"Who?"

"Simone. I know her from somewhere," she answered with the oddest look on her face. She looked confused, but determined; like she was certain that she knew what the fuck she was talking about.

"From where?"

"I don't really know. Can't put my finger on it."

"Maybe she just has a familiar face."

She thought for a second and then let it go. "Maybe so."

Then I couldn't help but check Eboni out. I wasn't lusting after her. I was just taking her in because, like I said, she reminded me of a yesterday that I wanted to go back to so desperately. I would have paid any amount of money and given my life over and over again just to go back to the days that I was in that two flat listening to Aeysha nag upstairs while Eboni's kids ran rampant downstairs against an old noisy wood floor.

Eboni shied away from my stare. "Sorry for just popping up."

"It's cool. It's actually good to see you. How you been?"

With a heavy sigh, she replied, "I'm making it. I can't complain."

I couldn't help but notice how thick she was. She was always thick than a motherfucker, but she had obviously put on a few more pounds.

"You thick as hell. You pregnant again?" I laughed to let her know that I was being playful.

"Whatever," she replied with a forced laugh.

"How did you know where I lived?"

"Just asked around the hood. You changed your number."

"Yea, I did. I'm sorry. I meant to give it to you before I moved."

Eboni sighed and pulled an envelope out of her purse. "Here. I printed out some pictures of Aeysha that I had in my phone. I thought you might want them."

I could see tears of sorrow in Eboni's eyes. She was doing a bad job of fighting them back. She took Aeysha's death just as bad as I did. Despite the bullshit that she and I were on, she loved Aeysha and I know she did. Her lust for me just led her to do some dirty shit that she regretted to that day. Guilt and regret was all over her face. She still mourned Aeysha's death, and she still mourned her own self respect that was lost when she played her friend so dirty.

I mourned the same.

"How is Dahlia doing?"

I had been so transfixed in this temporary trip back to the past that Eboni's presence was taking me on that I almost forgot my fucked up present.

I hated to tell her. I put my hands in my pockets. I rocked back and forth trying to soothe my own grief. "She passed."

"What?!" Eboni was beside herself.

The tears that once teetered at the doorway of her eyelids fell out. I reached out and hugged her. I held her tight. Her cries were muffled into the leather of my Moncler coat.

"What happened?"

"Crib death," I reluctantly told her.

I let her go and reached into my pocket for my phone. After going into the photo gallery, I began to show Eboni the hundreds of pictures that I had of Dahlia.

"Oh my God," she said with an amazed and adoring grin. "She had your eyes, but she looked just like Aeysha."

"Yea, she did. She was beautiful."

"Can you send me some of those?"

"Sure. Here."

I handed her my phone and let her go through the pictures and send them to herself as we caught up and talked. She caught me up on what was happening with folks I knew on the block that I once lived on. She told me about the bad ass kids that moved above her in my old apartment. She shared with me how her kids were doing, how they were growing up so fast and often asked about me and Aeysha.

We talked until snow began to fall and we were

forced to take cover. I walked her to her car, honestly feeling like I didn't want her to leave. Like I said, she put me in the mind of Aeysha.

I just didn't want that feeling to leave.

SIMONE

Shit! Shit! Shit!

I was in the house freaking the fuck out! My hands were literally shaking as I hoisted myself up on the back of the couch to look out of the window.

I frantically watched Omari and Eboni's exchange from the living room window. All the while I kept trying to ensure that Capone was still in the kitchen, unable to see how I was literally freaking out.

I wondered if Eboni remembered me from that day at Leona's. Though my hair was different, she looked at me like she thought I was familiar.

When I would hear Capone coming, I would go back to packing the box on the couch with Omari's clothes.

Once Omari walked her to the car, I got so anxious. My heart beat so nervously that my blood pressure skyrocketed to the point that my chest got tight. If Omari found out about me going to Leona's that day, so many cans of worms would open that I could never manage to close with even the most imaginative lie that I could come up with.

"Hey, baby." When Omari came into the living

room, I realized that he wasn't upset, at least not at me, so I figured that Eboni didn't recognize me after all.

"You okay?" I met him in the middle of the floor and put my arms around him.

"Yea, I'm good. It was just a lot seeing her."

"I'm sure it was."

"Are you almost done? I'm ready to get out of here."

Of course, Omari had been in the worst mood for the last couple of days. I was happy for him that he managed to come out of the house that day.

"Yea. I got most of the clothes you wanted."

"What should we do about Dahlia's services?" He was in a daze as he sat on the couch. He hadn't even heard a word that I said.

I sat beside him answering, "Whatever you wanna do, babe. What is it that you want to do?"

"I don't want a funeral service. Is that bad?"

There was so much sorrow in those beautiful gray eyes. I looked into his eyes feeling as if I would stop at nothing to make sure that I was the person that put happiness back into his spirit.

"It's not bad if that's what you want."

"I can't sit through another funeral," he said fighting tears.

"I know, baby."

"Can you take care of everything? I can't…"

I cut him off before his emotions took him to a place of no return. "I got you, baby."

He took deep breaths and fought the sorrow. He was so strong. His strength made me fall in love with him even more. "Make sure she gets buried as close to Aeysha as possible. Get her a nice pretty headstone."

"Consider it done."

Then, for the first time since finding out that I was pregnant, he reached over and touched my stomach. He caressed my stomach, squatted, and kissed it through my Chanel sweater.

My heart melted.

Finally, he was all in. He was where I needed him to be. I finally had security. Finally, it was all about me and mines. But I still wasn't pregnant. At that point, even if he got me pregnant, I wouldn't deliver on the necessary due date. Omari thought that I was almost three months pregnant at that point. Even if I got pregnant that day, I couldn't reasonably deliver in six months. I had even gone as far as taking prenatal vitamins every morning, which luckily made me throw up if I took them on an empty stomach. I needed to have a baby. The look in his eyes as he touched my stomach validated so much for me. Finally, I had that security. I was the only woman.

But with the timing being off, I didn't know where that baby was going to come from. Yet, it had to come from somewhere. I didn't have an option. I was so obsessed with making this work. I would have his baby. I just didn't know how.

CHANCE

I had been at Gia's crib all day. After weeks of hustling non-stop my body crashed and I slept most of the day.

Waking up with my hand on the curve of Gia's back and her weave in my face was a smack of reality. It was crazy how many turns my life had taken within the last couple of months. I went from a ward of the state, to a killer, to homeless and broke, to hustling aside major dope boys and fucking the baddest stripper in Chi Town's most popular strip club.

Even though things were looking up, I still felt like shit every time I thought about Simone. The way that she was treating me was really fucking with me. She still hadn't reached out to me since the day she came to the hotel and dropped that grand on me. I wanted answers. I needed this stupid and insecure feeling that was hovering over me every day to go away. And only she could make it go away by giving me some fucking answers. So when Gia got out of bed to take a shower, I called Simone.

I was obsessed with making this bitch fess up to her bullshit. All I needed her to tell me was that she used my goofy ass, because ignoring me like I was irrelevant was pissing me the fuck off.

After six rings, I got her voicemail.

I called again.

I could hear the shower running over my anger. My anger was fueled by visions of seeing that girl's body fall, fueled by memories of coming to the horrible realization that I had just shot a woman that was very much pregnant, and fueled with the immense disgust for Simone that I felt when I saw nothing but satisfaction on her face as she watched her lie on the ground bleeding to death until a neighbor came out to her car and saw her laying there.

After three rings, I got the voicemail. I was obviously sent to voicemail, so I called right back. I just wanted the bitch to acknowledge me, to acknowledge the fact that she fucked up my life without a care in the world, to acknowledge that she'd tricked me into killing a chick that probably had done none of the things she'd claimed she had.

"Stop calling me!!"

Simone caught me off guard when she answered.

She definitely threw me for a loop when she screamed at me like I was a terrorist.

"Stop fucking calling me, fucking stalker! I got a man!"

Then, she hung up.

OMARI

"We can't just keep fucking with him, boss. Either we gone kill him or lay off."

Nonchalantly, I chuckled as Capone and I stood in the back yard of the spot out south. Of course, Capone was smoking a blunt full of loud, despite already popping a molly.

While I never did any narcotics, Capone did enough for the both of us, I swear.

"If you're scared, go to church."

Capone laughed like I'd told the joke of the century; like Kevin Hart himself had his little ass in the backyard with us doing his best stand up.

"Scared? Nah. Neva scared. Just ready to get shit crackin'. Fuck them dirty ass niggas."

I leaned against the brick of the building as I hid behind the collar of my Pelle. It was cold as fuck outside, but I was so out of it mentally that I was willing to suffer through it in order to get some air.

It was crazy how Dahlia's passing had gone straight over my head. Her death wasn't what had me shook. It was the fact that it didn't hurt that scared the fuck outta me.

Aeysha's murder was such a heartbreaking loss for me. I knew pain like no other. At that moment, I knew that I'd experienced the worst pain of my life when I buried her, because nothing was coming close to making me feel that way again.

I mourned my baby girl, but mourning for her mother still overshadowed anything that would let me cry for her. At the young age of twenty-eight, I was used to death. Unlike street niggas who were used to death and thought nothing of it because they felt like it came with the territory, I was used to tragic loses and devastating pain.

"It'll crack soon enough," I told Capone. "He'll come to me."

"He don't even know that it's us jackin' him."

"He will."

Initially, I banked on taking Ching for everything. I planned on his organization crumbling as a result of Ching not knowing who was disloyal and taking him for everything. Then, I planned for him to hear through the streets how I was coming up heavy out south and putting two and two together; that his "nephew" was robbing him blind. He would then know that this was war because I knew that he'd killed Ayesha and would know that robbing him was first, but death was next.

Yet, the only part of that plan that had actually formulated was Ching assuming that somebody in his camp was robbing him. Capone still had connections out west that told him everything. Too scared to kill and end up back in the joint, Ching was whooping niggas asses and taking names left and right trying to figure out who was taking his shit.

"Real talk, we are risking our lives and our business. We start playing these games and niggas gone wanna retaliate. What if they hit us and take our stash? What if they ain't so careful about killing a nigga as we are? I know you wanted a war, but this ain't no war. You just fuckin' with him."

"And I'mma keep fuckin' with him until I'm ready to pop his ass."

Though he looked at me like I was crazy and shook his head in the same manner, he simply replied, "A'ight, boss."

I knew that Capone thought I was crazy. He thought I was losing it. But he was loyal, so he just had my back while I ran rampant.

"I don't know what I'm doing, no lie," I confessed. "I'm all over the place, but can you blame me?"

With smoke spilling from his nose and sympathy

pouring out of his eyes, Capone told me, "Nah, man. I can't blame you."

It was crazy how even though Capone knew that the shit I was doing didn't make any sense and was risky, he still had my back. For that, I was more careful with the decisions that I made because I was more careful with his life than my own.

GIA

♫ *Clappers to the front, front, front, front*
Clappers to the front, front, front, front
Shawty got a big ol' butt
Oh Yeeeeeah!!! ♫

The DJ had played "Clappers" just for me, so I was on the stage getting it! That night, I chose to be the "girl next door". Therefore, I was on stage on all fours bouncing my ass vigorously in simple black "Red Bottoms" and a black lace lingerie Vickie Secret set. Topped with garters, thigh highs, and a high bun, I looked like I had dressed up for my man and was dancing for him in our bedroom on Valentine's Day.

But the real scene was nothing of the sort. The stage was surrounded by an entourage of white businessmen who were clearly from out of town. They were older, mid to late forties, with salt and pepper hair cut into styles that caused hair to fall into their faces. Their faces were drenched with sweat caused from the tension of watching black ass all night. Their money was money. So I shook my ass like there was no tomorrow. I bent over in front of one, putting my mouth over the crotch of his Dockers, while another made it rain continuous dead men on my backside.

♫ *Got ass for days, come activate*
This ass on fire evacuate
Throw that ass in the air, evaporate
Where your money little bitch? Evaluate
If you got big money elaborate
I'mma shake this ass 'till I graduate ♫

Nicki Minaj's verse encouraged a twerk session like no other. I popped my ass vigorously as the song left the speakers.

"Yea, baby!"

The white men called out for me in lustful spurts.

"Damn, that ass is beautiful!"

Reluctantly, I had to leave the stage and all that white money. Yet, many of them requested private dances as me and the bouncer quickly collected my tips while the next dancer climbed onto the stage.

I had so many tips that I had to stash them away before giving private dances. I wanted to check my phone for messages from Chance anyway. So, while holding my singles and bra and panties that I had stripped away, I made my way to the dressing room.

I fought my way through the crowd of men, jealous that I had given all of my attention to the white men. They pulled at me and smacked my ass. Luckily, I had long since become accustomed to the disrespect and had grown a thick skin against ignorant drunk motherfuckers.

However, one person grabbed my arm so hard that I damn near fell to the floor. We caught eyes, and my heart fell to my chest in disappointment.

"What the fuck, Rae?! Let me go!"

This was such typical Rae! But I thought she'd gotten over this shit. Though she still called me and sent text messages frequently, she hadn't popped up since she walked in on me and Chance.

"I need to talk to you."

But I guess, since I had been ignoring her calls for the past three days, she decided that popping up was necessary.

Reluctantly, I allowed her to follow me towards the dressing room. I stopped right outside of the dressing room door. The walls were thicker, so some of the music was blocked and we could hear each other a little more clearly.

"What the fuck is your problem?! Stop putting your motherfuckin' hands on me!" I fussed as I fought to hold my tips while putting back on my panties and bra.

Rae sighed heavily and ran her fingers through her dreads. I could tell that our break up had gotten to her. She looked smaller, as if she had lost a few pounds. Her clothes weren't put together well. The color in her hair needed a touch up.

"I miss you, babe." As she spoke she reached for one of my hands as she wiped fallen tears away. Patrons, on their way to the bathroom, and dancers, on their way into the dressing room, looked on curiously. Some of the dancers knew me, so they knew Rae, and they snickered as they watched our exchange. I cringed in embarrassment.

"Rae, I can't do this right now. I am at work."

"Just listen to me, please." She was so sincere. Her face was wracked with pain and heartbreak. My heart went out to her. I didn't want to break her heart. I didn't want to be the source of the pain evident in her tired eyes.

But I didn't love her anymore.

"You're all I have. You are all I have had for a very long time." Tears were streaming so fast at this point that she didn't even fight to wipe them away. "I can't live without you. My life is so empty."

These were the same words that she left on my voicemail time and time again. These were the same words that she sent via text message over and over again. I felt sorry for Rae. I knew her life. I knew that without me she felt like an outcast. But every time I woke up without a burden on my chest, every time I woke up to Chance's arms around me, I knew that breaking up with her was right for me.

Now she had to do what was right for her.

"Rae, we can't stay together because your life is empty. Get out there. Find friends. Go link back up with your family. Mend that relationship. Date."

"I don't want to."

"You have to!" I screamed, flailed my arms, and kicked my legs so much that my heels crashed against the old beat up laminate flooring. "You have to, Rae. You cannot cling to me for the rest of your life."

She glared into my eyes as she finally wiped her face free of the sea of pain. In her eyes I saw all kinds of emotions; confusion, hurt, pain and anger.

She was lost, but I was no longer willing to help her find her way.

TEN

OMARI

A few days later, things went down exactly how Capone told me they would. For days, Ching sent word through the streets that he'd caught wind that I was the one hitting up his spots. Capone said that was it; it was time to stop playing with these niggas and get rid of Ching, and whoever else I saw fit that were responsible for Ayesha's death.

But before I could formulate a plan, before I could find this nigga, he found us.

Capone and I were standing outside of the spot out south, rapping with one of the block boys, Ringo. Suddenly, amid rotation of the blunt between Capone and Ringo as we talked numbers, we heard a screeching sound coming toward us from the end of the block. A white Tahoe came barreling towards us at sixty miles an hour down the residential block. Through the snowflakes that gently fell, I could see the smoke from the exhaust of the truck coming towards us like a heavy deathlike fog.

"Drive by!"

I barely heard the block boy over the sounds of the tires against the pavement; over the screams of the children that were throwing snowballs next door to us. I was mesmerized; watching them run in what seemed like slow motion towards their house.

I could feel somebody pulling me towards the building as the Tahoe approached. It slowed down to the point that it was crawling while the passenger side window slowly slid down.

People scattered like roaches; all except me, Capone, and Ringo. We stood behind trees and brick walls, aiming and exchanging fire with the Tahoe. Shots fired through the air. Sparks from our weapons illuminated the air like innocent fireflies detonating deadly bullets meant to kill.

It felt like the exchange lasted for hours. As I shot into the Tahoe, I wished that Ching was inside; riddled with every bullet from my Glock. Visions of Aeysha clouded my head and were motivation for me to continue to shoot through the cramp in my trigger finger.

What felt like hours were actually only seconds. It took not even a minute for gunfire to interrupt the peaceful solace of this hood on a cold winter day. The Tahoe's tires screeched as it took off. Me, Capone, and Ringo ran for our rides for an escape before the police arrived. As I climbed into the driver's seat, I frantically looked around for anybody struck by our bullets, but, thankfully, saw nothing but nosy eyes peering from windows and doorways.

We weren't worried about snitches. We fed that block. We housed homeless teens in that trap house. We gave crack heads odd jobs for cash. We gave the children ice cream cones in the summer and helped their mothers pay the heat in the winter.

The hood loved us and knew what came with the territory.

"Told you them niggas was on us," Capone said through heavy breaths as I weaved through traffic.

I was headed back to the spot in Riverdale.

The block boy was long gone in his '94 Cadillac.

"I believed you."

With a sly smile, he asked me, "Can we please kill these niggas now?"

It was an easy question to ask. Yet, for some reason, when for weeks I'd salivated at the thought of putting a bullet in Ching's head and every cavity in his body, I was hesitant to answer. After that quick moment of gunfire, I realized the capabilities of another body dropping that wasn't meant to. Ringo was an eighteen year old and the father of two. Capone, though childless, was young and full of ambition that was going to put him on so many levels as he climbed the ranks in the streets.

Had Ringo or Capone died during that exchange, it would have taken a piece of my heart, when I had a piece left only big enough to keep it beating.

"C'mon, boss. It's time," Capone convinced me. "It's either pop this nigga or keep having gunfights like we in the Wild Wild West. Next time somebody gon' get hit. And, I don't know about you, but I like being on this side of the grave getting money. You started this shit, now let's finish it."

He was right. Though I was enjoying fucking with this nigga for weeks and making rack after rack off his product, it was time to make Ching pay permanently for what he'd done. It was time to stop playing these childish little dope boy games and be the G' that I suddenly was.

"A'ight, man. Let's do this."

SIMONE

For the second time within a year, I was at a gravesite watching someone being lowered into the ground that I played a major part in putting there.

Only this time, Omari wasn't with me.

He couldn't stand to watch Dahlia being buried. He didn't want funeral services or a public burial. Against his family's wishes, against his mother's continuous pleas for a chance to say goodbye, he insisted that I just make this all go away as quick and painless for him as possible.

I did as I was told; found Dahlia a resting place close to Aeysha's. They were within three feet of one another, laying diagonally with each other in the earth.

Chills ran through me as Dahlia's small silver metal coffin was lowered into the frozen dirt. It was adorned with a beautiful bouquet of white roses and misty blue limoniums, her birth flower, per Omari's request.

Even after Tammy, even after Aeysha, I still surprised myself with the lengths I would go to be someone of significance in this man's life. The level of desperateness within me scared the shit out of me. I could still feel the biting cold of the patio door handle in my bare hands as I snuck back into my condo after watching Tiana's boyfriend go in shortly after Tiana thought I'd left that night. They were so busy smoking weed and listening to loud music that they didn't even hear my footsteps as I tiptoed back into the house, through the kitchen, and into Dahlia's room.

I stood before her crib and pondered what I was about to do for so long that it was amazing that Tiana never caught me in there. I was waiting for something in me to snap and tell me that what I was doing was insane. But all I could hear were Omari's constant loving words for Dahlia that overshadowed anything he felt for me or my unborn child.

Dahlia's autopsy would take weeks. But I was sure to make it look like just what they assumed it was; crib death. The investigation into Tiana and her boyfriend in relation to the child abuse was heavy.

As I stood in three inches of snow in red Giuseppe nappa boots, my cell phone began to belt out its ringtone. The bells and whistles ricocheted off of the trees in the quiet cemetery.

It was Chance, so I ignored the call.

I ignored the call, but I couldn't ignore the gnawing feeling in my stomach where a baby should be. Chance just would not go away. For every stunt I pulled, for every life I took, there was constantly something or someone in the way of my happily ever after.

Watching the coffin being lowered deeper and deeper into the ground, I replayed Omari's loving touches on my belly a few days before. I closed my eyes and engulfed myself in that love, realizing again that it was all for the best. The lengths I'd taken, the schemes, the lies, the murders; it was all for the best.

No ordinary woman would understand. No typical woman easily settled into a life with a committed loving husband would ever know the desperate need to be loved. No wife would know the feeling of always coming second. No beautiful woman would ever know the feeling of being looked over and passed up.

I didn't expect anyone to understand. That's why I kept my secrets buried inside of me under the comfortable notion that I had done it all for the best; for my best.

I stood there, finally the only woman that mattered in Omari's life.

CHANCE

"Man, Omari must really fuck with you if he wants me to bring you to his crib."

I shook my head as Capone tried to pass me the blunt while I drove down 94-East. No matter how many times I told him that I didn't smoke, he always offered.

"I keep telling you, I don't smoke," I told him with a chuckle.

"How could you not smoke? Drugs are great." We broke out laughing as he continued. "I see why Omari don't smoke, pretty boy ass. But you, I figured you a smoker."

"Naw, drinking is my thing. Besides, we weren't allowed to do drugs in the home. So I guess that shit just stuck with me. Now drinking is my shit."

"I feel you. Well anyway, like I was saying, Omari must really fuck with you. He don't want nobody knowing where his family lay their heads."

"Right. You told me that before. Something about a situation that happened in the past."

"Yea. Fuck niggas killed his girl." Capone's facial expression suddenly changed. I saw deep sadness in the eyes of a nigga that usually always had a happy drug induced grin on his face.

"Damn. For real?"

"Don't tell him I told you. I guess since he fucks with you, one day he will tell you himself. But yea, this nigga thought he snitched so he popped his girlfriend a few months back."

"Damn. That's fucked up."

I figured this game was pretty cut throat. I was raised deep in the middle of the trenches of the hood. I had been hearing about unforeseen tragic murders since I was able to comprehend English. Those tragedies ran across my mind often now that I was on the streets hustling; especially since I myself had murdered somebody in cold blood. I figured that at some point, I was going to reap what I sowed.

But I was willing to endure all of it to keep my pockets fat. Things had been so gravy for me since I started trappin'. I was pushing my own whip, splurging on Gia a lil' bit, and even paid a few of her bills so that I could keep comfortably sleeping there when I wanted to.

"What's this all about anyway? Do you know?"

Capone shrugged his shoulders as smoke escaped his mouth and filled the car with the smell of ganja. "I don't know. He might want us to make a run or some shit.

Who knows?"

As I drove towards the Roosevelt exit, it excited me that Omari thought enough of me to pull me in on whatever he had in mind. For years, even while living in Lexington House, I didn't know how my future would look. Even as I roamed the streets in Minnesota with twenty five grand in my pocket, I was worried about what my future held; if anything. Now, being alongside Omari and Capone, gave me some hope for a future, a lucrative one at that. It wasn't the most ideal choice for a career. It wasn't the safest or the most concrete either. But it gave me things that I never had before in my entire life; money and family. I belonged somewhere, finally.

Rich Homie Quan had spit a couple of bars on his "Type of Way" joint by the time Capone directed me to Omari's condo downtown. We were able to park right in front of the building and hop out.

"You good, homie?"

I assured Capone that I was good. I know that he noticed the look on my face. It wasn't bad though. I was simply taking in my surroundings. This was how I someday wanted to live, maybe even with Gia; in a beautiful neighborhood with our flashy cars parked in front of a multi-million dollar building that we lived in together.

That was the life. I was ready to live it. I was making my way there, one bag of heroine and one molly at a time.

Capone and I were buzzed in and, once going through the security door, were at Omari's condo that was on the first floor. The door was left open. I could hear two voices as he and I entered the kitchen.

Omari was standing behind, who I assumed was, his girl who stood at the kitchen sink washing dishes. He kissed her neck and smacked her ass right before noticing that we walked in. I heard him speaking but I was too focused on his girl to pay attention to what he was saying. I shook his hand while being mesmerized by his girl. Her ass was off the chain, but it wasn't its voluptuousness that had me mesmerized. It was its familiarity that had me shook. As she turned to face us, its familiarity hit me like the butt of a pistol crashing on the side of my head.

I was stuck and everyone noticed it, while Simone tried to front like she didn't know me.

"Nice, ain't she?" Omari stood proudly by Simone with his arm around her and an arrogant grin. "Now stop staring at my lady."

Simone didn't even fucking flinch! But she quickly got the fuck outta there.

"You stupid, baby," she told Omari with a giggle. Then she walked out of the kitchen as fast as she could.

Even Capone noticed how she belted out of the kitchen. "Well, damn. Hi, Simone!"

I was stuck. Rage filled my body so much that the surface of my skin was covered in heat and goose bumps. I couldn't even hear what Omari and Capone were talking about. I just followed them as they walked out of the kitchen through the patio while fighting to keep my composure and putting all the pieces of the puzzle together in my head.

Their words went over my head as we stood on the patio. I tried hard to act like I was listening, but the only thing I heard were Capone's words in my head that he told me as we rode over there.

"This nigga thought he snitched so popped his girlfriend a few months back."

My body wanted to fall unconscious. The trees and air spun around my head in violent loops.

"Aye, Omari. Where is your bathroom?"

I barely heard his instructions before opening the patio door and going back into the condo. I was looking for Simone. I walked through the kitchen and passed a baby's room. I followed noise down the hallway. I passed the bathroom and came across a closed door. Without even thinking, I opened it and saw Simone pacing the floor.

"BITCH..."

Immediately, she quieted me with harsh whispers as she met me in the doorway. "Ssssh!! Would you shut the fuck up?!" Before I could say another word, she hit me with a ton of questions. "What are you doing here?! How do you know them?! How long have you been..."

"Fuck all that!" This crazy bitch had a lot of nerve to question me! "You lied to me! You fucking bitch! You tricked me! Was that his girl that I killed?!"

"Chance..."

Without even thinking, my hands were locked down tightly on her elbows, squeezing them until I felt her bones amongst my fingertips as I forced my way into her bedroom. "Was it?!"

She couldn't even answer me. Her fucked up facial expression was answer enough though.

"Chance, I'll fix it. I'll help you, I promise. Just please be quiet. Please calm down. Please."

Tears were in her eyes. All of a sudden, she wasn't being a heartless bitch. All of a sudden, she wasn't ignoring me. All of a sudden, she was all about helping me.

I was so disgusted with this miserable bitch that I

just threw her on the bed with all the strength I had in me. She bounced into the air when her body hit the mattress. She looked at me with shock and fear in her eyes.

"Bitch, I better hear from you. Soon."

ELEVEN

OMARI

First thing I did when I woke up was check my cell. Surprisingly, I had a call from Eboni. I figured she just wanted to catch up, so I told myself to holla at her later. Then I checked my text messages. I had a few from Capone, Chance, the block boys out south, and Eboni.

What Eboni's text message read alarmed the fuck outta me. It said that she finally remembered where she knew Simone from. She claimed that she saw her at a restaurant with Aeysha sometime before Aeysha got killed. She also said that Simone had a little conversation with them and introduced herself, but didn't give them the name Simone.

I could hear Simone in the kitchen and could smell the bacon, so I got up and went into the kitchen to see what the fuck this was all about.

"Good morning," Simone said, smiling at me from the stove.

It was the perfect sight for a man to see at nine in the morning; a thick chick with a phat ass in lace boy shorts standing over the stove holding a skillet. Simone was great at catering to me. Most chicks change up after you start living together. But not Simone. She was the same down ass chick that she was when we met; fucking when I say so, cooking when I say so, jumping when I say so.

She had been laying it on even thicker since Dahlia passed. I knew that she was worried about me jumping off of the deep end with depression. Thanks to her handling the services, I was able to move on by keeping positive memories of the short time I shared with Dahlia in my heart and keeping in mind that now Aeysha finally had the chance to hold her baby.

"I just got the weirdest text," I told her as I sat at the table. "Do you know Eboni? The chick I introduced you to the other day that was outside the spot."

She looked over her shoulder curiously and then put her attention back on the frying bacon. "No. Not that I know of. Why?"

"She told me the day that she was at the spot that you looked familiar. Now she's saying that you were at some restaurant with her and Aeysha one day."

"What?" Now she gave me her full attention. "She must have me mistaken for someone else. I don't know her, and I definitely never met Aeysha."

Looking at my phone, I read the text verbatim to Simone. "Call me. I know where I know Simone from. She kicked it with me and Aeysha at Leona's before. She didn't say that her name was Simone though. Something is up with that chick."

Simone and I were silent for a few seconds. We were both were pretty much stuck. I didn't get what was going on or if there was anything to what Eboni was saying.

"Is she hating a little bit?"

"What you mean?"

She turned back to the stove and started to flip bacon while saying, "I mean, she could be starting some shit because you moved on so fast after Aeysha."

That was possible. I mean, though she was pretty remorseful when I saw her, seeing me could have rekindled some of her fucked up ways that led her to play games to get the dick like she did before.

"Have you ever slept with her?" Now Simone was giving me her full attention again. Her arms were folded and she leaned against the kitchen sink still wearing the oven mitt. "Be honest."

"Hell naw."

Immediately, she smiled like she knew that I was lying. "Nigga, don't lie. I know you. Don't think I forgot how we met. Did you fuck her?"

Reluctantly, I nodded my head.

"Well then, there you go. That bitch is throwing salt on me."

I figured Simone was right. Hell, she didn't know the stunts Eboni pulled back in the day, but I did. She had the potential to do a number on Aeysha and that was supposed to be her friend. So, I was sure that there were no limits to what she would do to a chick with no connection to her that stood in the way of the dick she wanted.

Besides, there was no way that Simone would know who Aeysha was even if she had bumped into her in the past. I wasn't the type of nigga to pillow talk with my side bitch about my main bitch. Before Aeysha passed, Simone had never even seen a picture of Aeysha.

"Look, Omari. I don't have time to be going through what you put Aeysha through. I know that they say that you keep 'em how you get 'em, but I do not want you cheating on me."

Instantly, I stood in defense. I walked towards her and put my arms around her waist.

"You do not have to worry about that shit," I told her, kissing her lips.

She didn't. Real talk. I wasn't that man anymore. I

hadn't slept with another woman besides Simone since Aeysha was killed. My mistress was the streets. My side bitch was my mission to kill Ching.

I was carrying around enough guilt. I didn't have space for any more.

CHANCE

Me and Gia spent the day cuddled up on her couch. It was freezing outside; a mere ten degrees. There was another block boy on shift out in Riverdale, thank God, so I was posted with this pretty *older* thang.

Gia giggled as I nibbled on her neck. "Boy, stop. I'm trying to watch TV."

She was all into some reruns of Basketball Wives and I was all into her. I was drunk as fuck. Every since I ran into Simone, Grey Goose had been my best motherfuckin' friend. It was the only thing I could do to live with myself. The only way I could deal with what that bitch did was by being drunk.

I knew she killed that girl just for that nigga. I just knew it. I hadn't gotten the details from Capone on exactly how or when Omari's girl died, but Simone's face told it all. She had me kill that Omari's girl with some stupid ass lic about her brother. That bitch tricked the fuck outta me, and it drove me crazy just thinking about it.

"Chance, stop! Quit, boy!"

To make the repulsive thoughts go away, I tried to lose myself in Gia's cleavage. My tongue disappeared amongst her perfect perky 34 Cs. My hands cuffed soft booty cheeks that stumbled out of spandex boy shorts.

The doorbell rang and unfortunately fucked up a nigga's flow.

Immediately, Gia rolled her eyes dramatically into the back of her head. "Urgh."

It could have only been one person. Me and Gia knew that. She never had uninvited guests. In a neighborhood like hers, people didn't just ring your doorbell.

It was Rae. I fought to keep my amused laughter under wraps. Rae was not willing to let go. She had been blowing Gia's phone up heavy. I couldn't blame her. Gia was a beauty, and that pussy was addictive.

I'd be stalking too.

Gia fussed as she stood up to answer the door. "What this bitch want?!"

"You know what she wants! The same thang I'm gettin'," I said with a laugh as I playfully smacked her ass.

Gia ignored my flirtatious attempts. She was heated as her bare feet stomped out of the living room and towards the door. "This ain't funny!"

I could still hear her mumbling all kinds of curse words as she went down the hall to open the door. I didn't move a muscle. For one thing, I couldn't. The Grey Goose was making the whole room spin. I stayed stuck leaning sideways on the couch cushion.

But when Gia came stomping back into the living room with Rae following behind her like a puppy, I forced myself to get my shit together. Rae was a woman, but she most definitely thought she was a man. Just in case this chick wanted to run up because I had her girl, I wanted to be ready.

She didn't though.

"Chance, I'm just going to let her get some more of her things."

The fact that Gia explained herself to me threw Rae for a loop. It was like what little pride she had left flew out of the window as her chest sunk in disappointment. She looked Gia upside her head like she was crazy. But Gia ignored her like she meant nothing.

I simply said, "Cool," as they kept walking towards the bedroom.

As soon the bedroom door closed, all I heard was shouting.

"You love that nigga or something?!"

"It's not about that, Rae! I told you that! I don't want to be with you anymore. We are over!"

"But you're all I got! You're all I have! I'm out here with nobody!"

I felt sorry for buddy as I heard tears coming through her shouts. It was crazy to hear such a butchie ass chick shed tears like a bitch.

"I want you back! I want our family back!"

"We ain't got no family, Rae! You need to move on!"

Seconds later, the bedroom door slammed again. Then Gia appeared in the living room with frustration all over her face. She looked flustered and her caramel skin was even a little red. The situation was starting to sober me up. The look on her face when she walked in and the level of emotion I heard from her was enough for me to pay attention to what the fuck Rae was on.

She didn't just come here to pick up some clothes. She wanted her girl back.

"I'm sorry," Gia told me. "She will be gone in a few minutes."

"Did you know that she was coming over?"

"Of course not," Gia fussed as she frustratingly ran her fingers through her hair. "She used that as an excuse to get in. I am so sick …"

Pow!

A sudden and quick pop made me and Gia jump out

of our skin. We sat frozen with bulging eyes as we stared down the hallway.

Seconds went by without us hearing anything else. Finally, my instincts kicked in and I reached under the couch where I stashed the Glock that Capone gave me.

We sat still, damn near not even breathing, listening for further sounds, but heard nothing.

"What the fuck," finally left Gia's lips along with heavy breathing. "Rae! Rae!"

"Ssssh!" I quieted Gia as I slowly stood with my gun drawn.

When Gia stood as well, I told her to stay back. Of course, like a woman, she refused and was close behind me as I crept down the hallway.

Gia's bedroom door was still closed. It was quiet as hell besides my Timbs making sticky sounds against the oak hardwood flooring.

The more the silence filled the house, the more I realized what might have happened. Reluctance and fear filled my body as I slowly opened the bedroom door.

As soon as I saw Rae's body lying across the bed, with a gun in her hand and half of her head blown off to the other side of the bed and splattered all over the headboard, I quickly slammed the door closed.

"Oh my God! What happened?!"

Gia fought to get by me. But I stood firm, blocking her way into the bedroom, all while fighting the vomit attempting to come out of my mouth.

The sight of blood leaking from Rae's head and the sight of her skull in pieces was still embedded in my brain. I was already queasy from the abundance of Grey Goose. Now, I heaved in reaction to the sight of brain matter all over Gia's sheets.

SIMONE

Omari giggled as I pulled on his dick which was covered by silk boxers.

"Babe, stop. I gotta shower," he told me with a bashful grin.

"Well, hurry up. I want it." I literally was purring as I kneeled in the bed in front of him. He stood before me like a Greek god. His body looked better than ever. It amazed me how he stayed looking so edible. He was obsessed with his body looking good and it showed.

"I'll be back," he told me as he grabbed my chin gently. Then he kissed my lips so softly that my pussy leaked with appreciation. His lips were so soft and moist that I wanted to take them from him and keep them with me as he showered so that I could put them wherever I wanted to on my body.

His swagger as he left the room was so slow, calm, and confident. Even watching him walk away was a miracle of God. His back was sculpted better than any building on the Magnificent Mile.

No wonder I was losing my mind.

As soon as I heard the bathroom door close, I eyed

his cell phone on the nightstand. I jumped at it like a cat.

I knew his code after looking over his shoulder as he unlocked his phone so many times. I immediately went to his Google Play Store and downloaded Mr. Number Call Block.

I had to keep Eboni from calling him. This morning scared the shit out of me. Being in the same place as Aeysha was harmless. It's not like it would have led to revealing that I had anything to do with her murder. But I was so perfect in Omari's eyes. I didn't want this bitch coming into the picture and causing him to look at me sideways. I had gone too far and done too much to be in this flawless position. I didn't need this ghetto rat bitch coming out of nowhere with her little Inspector Gadget ass.

Things were unraveling like crazy! I had to snip the end soon before everything fell apart. Chance had me shook! I had to figure out how to get him away from my man and out of Chicago before his young ass did something stupid. He was so angry that he was willing to do something irrational just to get back at me. Omari could have easily heard his outburst that night in our bedroom.

I blocked Eboni's number as soon as the App was done downloading. While I was at it, I blocked his sister's number too.

I didn't want that bitch, Erica, anywhere in the picture off pure hate alone.

Omari wasn't technically savvy enough to even notice the App. I was the one that had to download Vine for him so that he could watch all those hoes show their pussy for free.

When Omari walked back into the room, completely dry, in a bath towel and smelling like Dove for Men, he hit me with another bombshell.

He dropped his towel, revealing a marvelously sculpted body and a beautiful penis surrounded by soft and clean shaven skin. He threw the towel across the room and climbed into the bed with me butt naked. Immediately, he spooned with me for warmth beneath our goose down comforter. When he instantly laid his hand on my belly, my heart melted but beat furiously with dread.

"When is your next appointment?"

I played it off. "Why? Are you actually going to go with me?"

He smacked his lips. "C'mon now. You know you always tell me last minute right when I'm in the middle of something. Last time, you didn't even tell me that you were going."

That was my only way to fool him. I lied about

doctor's appointment. I was currently feverishly trying to figure out how to get an ultrasound to show him eventually.

"Well, you're always so busy, baby."

"I want to go. I need to."

"Okay. I can't remember off hand when my next one is. I'll look at my calendar in the morning and let you know."

Things were unraveling before my eyes. The lies were unfolding so fast that I couldn't keep up. I was covering one lie up after another with more lies and more bullshit. Eboni, Chance, the pregnancy; all of it was coming at me at the speed of lightning that I was literally fumbling my way through my deception and lies.

TWELVE

OMARI

Two weeks after Dahlia was buried, I finally went by to see my mother.

I still hadn't visited Dahlia. I couldn't bring myself to do it. Subconsciously I felt like I would have to face Aeysha and explain to her why I had, once again, let her down.

But I was ready to face my mother. I had to. She was pissed that I didn't have any services for her grandbaby.

It broke my heart when she looked at me with disgust after opening the front door of her brick two story home in Tinley Park. She had a lot of nerve. She couldn't even afford the door that she barely wanted to open for me. I was in this shit because I'd put myself in harm's way just to keep this roof over her head.

She was also to blame for Aeysha's death, and she ain't even know it. No, she didn't pull the trigger and she didn't make me start hustling. But she put me under the pressure that I felt to make the money that got Aeysha killed.

I shook off the thought as I walked into my mother's house. It smelled of old Avon perfume and Skin So Soft. The smell burned my nose. I tried to hold my breath as I sat beside my mother on her sofa. Despite the smell, she looked good. My mother was still beautiful. Her eyes were big and deep like moons, matching its color. She was aging well. Despite natural crow's feet of a woman in her sixties, she could have easily passed for her early fifties. She kept herself up by walking on a treadmill that was in the corner of her living room facing the television. She stopped eating meat when she was in her thirties. She still had a great figure that could compete with a lot of chicks out here.

"Your sister has been trying to call you." She talked to me like she could barely stand it, like she hated that she had to.

"No, she hasn't. She on some bullshit anyway."

"What do you mean by that?"

My mother knew that I was in the drug game. I had no desire to ever hide it from her. If she wanted me to be able to help her financially, she had no choice but to accept how I got my money.

"Told Tre about my business. Simone heard the nigga talking about me while we were over there. She talks too much. I can't have that type of shit."

"Umph," was my mother's only response.

Besides being beautiful, she held a smug and disappointed look on her face. I could help her financially, but there was nothing I was willing to do to take that look off of her face. I had to do what was best for me.

When she noticed me noticing her, she spoke to me in a stern and hurt voice. "I can't believe you didn't let me say goodbye to my grandbaby."

"Mama, I don't want to talk about it."

"Well, I do!"

"But I don't, mama!"

She smacked her lips and blew her breath in disapproval. She shook her head in reprimand as she shifted her weight away from me. "You act like you're the only one going through this. Aeysha wasn't my girlfriend, but she was like a daughter to me and it hurt me too..."

"Mama, I do not..."

"Listen to me, damn it!" Her body shook as her voice escalated.

I laid my hand on her knee. "Calm down, mama."

"No! You need to calm down. You need to calm down, son."

I saw that she was upset. I saw that she was so

angry that her nerves were causing her to tremble. I couldn't take anything happening to my mother; not a heart attack, not a stroke, not even a cold. So, I shut up despite my insides burning with irritation.

I didn't want to hear this shit. I made it through the day without dwelling on Aeysha and Dahlia. She wanted to have a deep and heartfelt conversation about some shit that I couldn't handle. It was going to make her feel better by getting it off her chest, but I was going to walk out of there with an even heavier burden on my mind that would lead me to doing something bad- very bad.

"You ain't the only one dealing with death. You forget that I am your mother, so I feel your pain too. Aeysha was like a daughter to me. Don't forget, I was the last person that she talked to that day. She went outside because of me…"

The memory was so painful that my mother's tears came out in despair. She clutched her chest with one hand and covered her leaking eyes with the other. I hurriedly wrapped my arms around her and rocked her gently as soft wails escaped her mouth.

"It's okay, mama."

"I sent her outside."

"I didn't answer the phone," I said through my own

tears.

"Stop shutting me out, baby. Stop being so hard. I wanted to say goodbye to the only living memory of Aeysha. That was my first grandbaby. You took that from me."

"I'm sorry, mama." My voice cracked as my heart did as well. I allowed myself to cry and miss Dahlia just like she did. "I didn't say goodbye either. We can go say goodbye together, okay?"

She didn't respond. She just cried. She held me and just cried into my chest.

And I let her, while I allowed myself to shed stubborn tears of my own.

GIA

No matter how much Rae was irritating me, I could not believe that she was gone.

No matter our recent separation, she had been such a part of my daily routine. Even after we broke up, I had become accustomed to hearing her voice every day, even if it was her begging to get back with me or cursing me out for fucking with Chance.

"Where do you want these boxes?"

I told Chance to take the boxes of clothes to the second bedroom. From there, I planned to sort everything out and store what was needed in the closet of the master bedroom.

I was moving into a new house. After Rae's suicide, there was no way that I was going to keep living there. The day she shot herself, I left and had only gone back to pack. The bloody comforter was still on the bed, which stunk like a dead body. Evidence of the paramedics and coroner being in my bedroom was still sprawled everywhere.

Just the thought gave me eerie and horrified chills. I forced myself to focus on the box of kitchen appliances that I was unpacking. But it wasn't working. As I unpacked the electric can opener, toaster, and blender, Rae's dejected words rang in my head over and over again.

I felt so helpless. Initially, I felt so independent, as if I had to leave Rae for me. Now, I felt like I should have handled her with kid gloves. I knew her story. I knew that she was lonely. I knew that she had no one in her life like me.

Yet, I was so selfish and so dick-mitized that I was reckless with her heart. When I thought about my life before her suicide, I felt good about leaving her. I was free. I was light hearted. Chance had little to do with that, but he still added to the joy of my daily life.

Now, I wondered if it was all worth it.

I watched Chance walking around drunkenly; barely able to carry the boxes that he was transporting. I wondered was throwing him in Rae's face worth it. We weren't in a committed relationship. I was enjoying being single, and he was enjoying getting his life back in order. But we both were very real with each other about how much we liked each other. I was even throwing myself out on a limb by dating his young ass.

However, things had changed recently. I guess the sight of a woman with her head nearly blown off would put things into a different perspective for anybody. It was definitely putting things into a difference perspective for me; which was why I was wondering what was up with the sudden change that I was seeing in Chance.

All of a sudden, he was drunk most of the time. When he wasn't, he was short, bitter, and angry. Something was wrong with him, and it wasn't me. But I didn't sign up to be in another fucked up situation with a significant other. I didn't sign up to babysit another grown motherfucker with issues.

CHANCE

After leaving Gia's new crib, I headed over to the spot in Riverdale. My stomach was bubbling. I was nervous as fuck. A few weeks ago I was about this life. I was ready to do what the fuck I had to do to survive. But this; this was something I never wanted to do.

Not again.

Especially to somebody else that didn't deserve it.

All day, I'd tried to calm my nerves by drinking away the fear and dread that consumed me since me, Omari, and Capone had that talk outside his condo.

That shit wasn't working though.

As I road down 147th Street towards the spot, my cell phone rang. I was riding in silence; having a mental conversation with myself and my conscience. The bright lights of my cell and that screeching ringtone scared the fuck outta me.

I answered immediately when I saw that it was Simone.

"What's up?"

I hadn't talked to her since I saw her at the condo. Yet, she'd been texting me nonstop saying how she was going to fix this.

How was she going to fix something so fucked up was beyond me. But she was known to pull one hell of a rabbit out of her hat, so who knew what she would come up with.

"Where are you?"

"On my way to the spot."

She huffed and puffed. "You can't keep working for him."

"What the fuck am I suppose to do? Until you come up with some cash, I'm trappin'."

"Trap somewhere else!"

"Where?!"

Her smart ass didn't have an answer for that.

"Shit. Don't you think if I had an option, I would have been on it already?"

As always, she changed her tone. She was sweet, nurturing and somewhat lustful. She used the same tone while I was living in transitional housing, telling me that her brother's ex-wife was a dirty bitch taking him for everything and beating his daughter; a dirty bitch whose life was worth twenty-five thousand dollars that was supposed to change my fucked up life.

"You need to leave, Chance."

I laughed hysterically. "Shit, the way shit is going down, sounds like you need to leave too."

Silence.

"Oh, but I forgot. You jumped through so many hoops to get this nigga that you too sprung to leave."

It was funny how no matter how much proof I had, she still danced around her truth.

"This is cutting it too close. They are still investigating her murder."

That made the bubbles in my gut dance like the Twerk Team. I was wrong for killing Aeysha. I would probably kill myself with alcohol, then eventually drugs, by trying to float through the guilt.

But I be damned if I end up in prison for some shit that I was coerced into doing.

Simone took my silence as weakness, an opportunity to convince me. "You have to leave."

"I can't leave without any money. Set me up and I'll bounce."

I was willing to bounce. This shit was becoming too hectic. I needed to get the fuck away from these motherfuckers.

"I don't have any," she groaned.

"Well, find some." Then, I took her silence for

weakness. "I'm not leaving again without a cushion. Yea, I fucked up the first time, but I won't let it happen again. I understand you want me gone. Shit, I wanna be gone too. Shit is getting way to thick around here."

She chuckled sarcastically. "Hell, how can it get any thicker than this?"

I had an answer for her rhetorical question. "They're about to kill Ching."

"What?"

"Tonight. That's why I was at the condo that day. He wants to kill Ching. He thinks he killed Aeysha. I ain't for killing another innocent person. What the fuck am I supposed to do?"

Simone snuffed out my guilt. She caught how weak I was in this; how close I was to the edge. "Well, kill him!"

"What?!"

"Kill him! Do what the fuck you gotta do to keep yourself from looking suspect. He didn't kill Aeysha, but Ching has been in the game for years. Do you know how many people he probably killed?!"

Once again, I couldn't believe the pure audacity of this bitch. She was willing to do anything, take any steps, to keep this shit going. But everything she was doing, every step she was taking, was about covering her ass and to keep herself in a sweet position.

My heart was heavy. I was stuck in between a rock and a hard place. I didn't want to kill again. I didn't want innocent blood on my hands again. But I also didn't want these niggas looking at me suspect because I was bowing out.

As I pulled up in front of the spot, Capone and Omari were standing out front waiting on me. I knew that I had to do what I had to do.

"You have to go along with this. Otherwise they will suspect something," Simone told me, seemingly begging. "*Kill him.*"

OMARI

I expected to be reluctant.

I expected to be scared.

I expected to want to turn around.

But the closer we got to Ching's crib, I only felt assurance.

After visiting with my mother and seeing her pain, I wanted nothing else than to get rid of the man that did this to us. Sure, I played a big part in it all, but I was spending every day of my life killing myself slowly.

Chance drove the beater as we coasted down the e-way. He was silent and looked focused. I figured Capone and I needed an extra hand. I didn't know who would be at Ching's crib or how many. I immediately thought of Chance. Though new to the game, out of all the block boys, he seemed the smartest and most dedicated. He was focused. He had the same struggles as I did when I got in the game. He wasn't just some young nigga trying to serve because he thought it was cool. He was out there to survive.

His hustle was real.

We pulled into the alley behind Ching's crib. From being in there hundreds of times, I knew we could get in through the back door. I didn't want him to see me coming. I knew that if he did, there would be heavy gunfire exchanged. I just wanted this shit to be quick and easy in order to keep any harm from coming to Capone and Chance.

I salivated at the thought of watching Ching die. It excited me that I was going to be able to look him square in the eye when I pulled the trigger. I wanted to be so close to him when he died that the splatter of his blood mixed with my sweat.

The snow and ice made crunching noises beneath our boots. It was two in the morning, so it was quiet as hell outside. Capone and Chance followed me like obedient and loyal soldiers as we crept through the backyard towards the back door.

I had it all planned out, so there was no need for us to make a sound. As soon as we reached the back door, I shot two bullets through the keyhole. After throwing the door open, I ran up the back steps and kicked down the door that lead to his kitchen. The house was pitch black and quiet. I wasn't expecting that. Ching basically stayed up twenty-four hours a day, and Capone had gotten word from his dip from the West Side that one of her friends was fucking Ching and with him that night. She even called Capone earlier and told him that her girl was texting her from Ching's crib.

That's when we decided to make the move.

But as I walked through the crib, I noticed that, besides it being dark, it was pretty empty. I went into Ching's bedroom and noticed that his TV was gone. I opened drawers and saw that clothes were missing.

"Shit."

Capone and Chance realized the same shit that I did.

"He bounced," Capone said with a laugh. "This nigga ran."

Chance stood at the door, gun still in hand, finger still on the trigger. "What you wanna do?"

They both stood staring at me waiting on instructions that I didn't have. It was crazy how disappointment consumed me to the point that I couldn't think. That night was supposed to be the night. It was supposed to be over with the pull of a trigger. The burden was going to be lifted. The hate was going to be out of my heart. I was supposed to be able to start living again.

When it was supposed to be over, things were feeling like they had just begun.

THIRTEEN

GIA

I rolled over the next morning with attempts to get things back to normal. It had been a couple of days since I moved into my new place. The house smelled new; like fresh paint. The sheets were new and fresh. The down comforter kept me and Chance warm and cozy.

I knew that he was awake. He had been tossing and turning all night and morning for some reason. He was still in a funky mood and lying to me; saying that nothing was wrong.

To make us both feel something close to normal, I sensually crawled on top of him. Between my legs was a morning wood strong enough to knock my teeth out. I slid down on it slowly. As I did so, our eyes met. The chemistry that shot through my body when we stared into each other's eyes was missing like a late period.

However, my pussy still leaked naturally in anticipation of his dick being inside of me. I was able to easily slide down on it once on my tip toes.

As I rode him, we both made soft lustful sounds, but

something was definitely different. There was tension between us. There was no excitement in our horny moans. The lust that was once there was replaced with strain and pressure similar to a couple that had been together for ten years.

I even felt his dick losing an erection amongst my walls. At first, I tried to keep riding him, hopping up and down slowly, in hopes that it would encourage his dick to come back and play. But that wasn't working. Slowly, his erection ran out of the room, like it was a scared little boy, until the point that his dick was falling out of me.

I didn't give up though. Things had to get back to normal. Being with Chance had to work.

I wanted the happiness back that I felt just a few weeks ago. We weren't in love and my life wasn't perfect, but being happy again would make me feel like I was right for leaving Rae. At first, I was so justified for being selfish and moving on. Yet, her death had me rethinking every choice that I made these last couple of months.

Her death was on my conscience.

I disappeared underneath the covers and came face to face with his dick. I was so let down when my eyes met it and saw that it was lying nonchalantly and lackadaisically on his thigh.

I began to bathe it with spit and lust, but it still lay lifeless inside of my mouth.

I knew I had a good head game. If anything, I was a beast at sucking dick. On many occasions, Chance fought hard to keep from cumming prematurely in my mouth. My mouth was like a Jacuzzi. There was no reason for his dick not to be appreciative of the attention my mouth was giving it.

When I came up from underneath the covers, Chance saw the irritation on my face.

"Why you stop?"

I looked at him like he was crazy. "Because yo' dick ain't hard! Urgh!"

"Get it hard then. Why you gettin' so mad?"

I huffed and puffed while lying back down. "Because since when do I have to 'get it hard'? That motherfucka usually stay hard. What's wrong with you?"

He tried to smirk and chuckle like I was the one with the problem. "Nothing. Shit, I was enjoying the head."

Overcome with frustration, I sat up and looked at him. Just like a man avoiding the issues, he grabbed me gently and attempted to pull me back down on top of him.

"No, Chance! Stop."

I was literally fighting back tears. Mind you, I was

probably overreacting, sensitive after seeing my ex blow her head off in my bedroom. But I was not just tripping. Something was wrong with Chance.

I just knew it.

"Talk to me. What's wrong?"

"Nothing. I told you I was enjoying the head. Come back over here." Again, he reached for me and I slapped his hand away.

"No, you weren't. And I don't mean right now. I mean what's wrong with you period. You've been huffing and puffing. You walk around here angry with a fucked up attitude like I did something to you. And we ain't even fuckin'."

We hadn't had sex since Rae committed suicide. I understood it the first two weeks, but after so long I figured it was weird. Hell, I should have been the one sad and not wanting to fuck. Not him.

"Man, I told you ain't nothing wrong with me. I'm gucci."

I smacked my lips and threw my hands in the air. "I didn't sign up for this shit."

"Sign up for what?"

"I went from one fucked up relationship to another. We ain't even in a committed relationship and the shit done turned bad already."

"Gia, I told you I'm straight."

"And I'm telling you that you're not. I may not know you that well, but I know you well enough to know when you actin' funny. Something is bothering you and it's fucking up the flow of what you had goin'. I'm not happy."

Chance tried to convince me, but I wasn't buying it. "I'm good."

"You told me that we would always keep it real with each other."

He had. Many times, we talked about how I had so many trust issues with men because of my past. Every time, he promised that he was different.

He replied, "I am," but something wouldn't allow his words to convince me.

I left the bed. I couldn't stand looking at that nigga no more, so I went into the kitchen in deep thought.

This was for the birds. All I could think about was how I treated Rae, how I hurt her by throwing him in her face.

Every time the thought crossed my mind, my heart broke more and more.

OMARI

I woke up to sounds of Simone heaving in the bathroom. Her morning sickness was worse than Aeysha's. Like clockwork, she threw up every morning before taking her shower while getting ready for work.

She was about five months at this point. Finally, I was getting excited about having a baby. Since Dahlia's death, I was missing the sound of a baby's cries and the smell of baby lotion.

As Simone walked into the bedroom wearing her robe and rubbing her stomach with an uncomfortable frown, I noticed how I was finally looking at her differently. She wasn't just my woman. She was the mother of my child. She had gained only a few pounds. She had a small bulge that was just now starting to poke out.

"You okay?"

Simone smiled at me while sitting at her vanity. While taking the satin cap off her head and allowing her long weave to fall twenty-two inches down her back, she answered, "I'm fine. I just hate throwing up."

"Did you reschedule your appointment yet?"

Simone was scheduled for a prenatal appointment

last week that got canceled because her doctor had a family emergency in California. She didn't want to see a different doctor, so opted to reschedule her appointment. I was a little let down because I had yet to be able to go with her to an appointment, so I made sure that I was free and available to go with her that day. I was looking forward to seeing my baby in the same 3D ultrasound that I'd seen Dahlia on so many times before finally seeing her face to face.

"No, not yet. I'll do it today though."

"My mama told me the other day that Erica is having a boy. I know she's happy as hell. That's what she wanted."

As she flat ironed her hair, I caught Simone roll her eyes hard as hell. Every since she heard that shit Tre said about me, she hated even talking about my sister. It didn't matter to me. I mean, I was mad about the same shit, but Erica and I didn't fuck with each other like that anyway. So it didn't bother me.

"She's going to have to have a c-section though. She got diabetes, or some shit my mama was saying." Now I was just fucking with Simone by continuously talking about Erica. I liked to see her turn up her nose. I liked that bougie shit about her, especially when she hated a motherfucka just because of me. That's that loyalty that made me fall for her.

"That's interesting," Simone replied nonchalantly. "Anyway… What do you want us to have?"

"I don't care, baby. As long as it's healthy. Are you going to find out the sex of the baby at your next appointment?"

"I'm not sure if I am far enough along for that."

"Aeysha was able to find out when she was…"

She put her hand up and cut me off with a stare that shut me completely up. "Don't compare me to, Aeysha." She was literally glaring at me.

"I wasn't. I was just sayin'…"

"Do not compare me to Aeysha!"

I stared at her from the bed, still under the comforter hiding from the cold morning air. "Whoa, baby. Calm down. Why you gettin' upset?"

"I'm sick of everything being about Aeysha. I expect you to mourn for her, but will it ever be about me? You walking around here mad because you're obsessed with Ching because of her. You can't even make an appointment with me because you so busy in the streets trying to find him. Now you're comparing my pregnancy to hers!"

I expected Simone to be sensitive about hearing

Aeysha's name. She knew that Aeysha was the woman that had my heart. She knew that if Aeysha was still alive, I would not be in that condo with her. I would be at home with the woman that I planned to live the rest of my life with. Therefore, Simone's taking offense to Aeysha's constant presence in this relationship didn't even upset me.

"I understand how you feel. I'll try not to mention her name around you. I don't want you to be upset, especially with you being pregnant and everything."

"But you're still going to kill Ching, aren't you?"

She'd completely stopped doing her hair and gave me her full attention.

"I'm not discussing that with you. I don't want you knowing anything about that. I don't want you involved."

"Too late, Omari! I already know."

"Well, you won't know anything else. I'm not discussing it. Period."

She called herself glaring at me like that shit was supposed to scare me, but I didn't give a fuck. I closed my eyes and got comfortable in a position that was not facing her. I was also very comfortable with spending most of my days finding Ching's ass.

SIMONE

About an hour before leaving work, I locked my office door and began to search online for 3D ultrasound pictures that I could manipulate and print on the glossy paper that I bought from Office Max on lunch.

I was desperate. This pregnancy scheme was unraveling along with every other lie, scheme, and move I'd pulled.

After searching Google, I was presented with hundreds of pictures that I could manipulate to my liking. All I needed to do was change the patient's name and doctor's name, after finding one that was the same amount of weeks that I was supposed to be.

Talking to Omari that morning caused an epiphany to hit me. I realized how I could successfully carry this pregnancy out and produce a baby. I just needed to come up with a plan to make it so that Omari missed the delivery.

I wasn't about to let things fall through the cracks. I had done too much to get where I was. I was his woman. I was the only woman. I wasn't sharing him with anyone. I had the position that I always wanted, and I wasn't about to let it go. Not for Aeysha. Not for Dahlia. And definitely not for Chance. So after successfully using Photoshop to add my information to the ultrasound picture, I printed it. Then I finally returned Omari's text from about an hour ago, asking how I was doing. I text messaged back, saying that I was sorry for taking so long to get back to him. I added that I was in the clinic with no reception since my doctor called and said that she was in town and had an available appointment for this afternoon if I wanted it.

I knew that he would be upset for missing yet another appointment, but I planned to go home and give him such a dick sucking spa treatment that he would forget all about it. Yet, fear that I wouldn't be able to continue to dance around these appointments gave me chills.

Of all the lies I'd told, of all the secrets I'd had, this was the most wretched and outlandish of them all.

Before slipping the ultrasound picture into an envelope, I looked at it and wished desperately that it was really Omari's baby that I was laying eyes on. However, I knew that I'd come up with the picture perfect plan to give him the baby that he was expecting.

I'd bought myself a little more time with that ultrasound. I felt much better than I did this morning sitting at the vanity literally with the bubble guts as I felt the walls crashing in on me. I was now leaving the office and heading to the parking lot feeling slightly better.

Full relief would come once I got Chance the fuck out of the picture. Like the baby, I had a plan in the works to accomplish that as well. So I headed towards the spot in Riverdale.

I text messaged Chance on my way there to make sure that he wasn't there. Then I confirmed that Omari was at home. Twenty minutes later, I was pulling up in front of the house. Fred, one of the block boys, was posted on the porch. For the life of me, I couldn't understand how these little boys stood outside in twenty degree weather all day.

"What's up, Simone?"

"Hey, baby."

"Omari isn't here."

"I know. I just wanted to grab some more of his things since I was in the area."

Fred opened the front door for me. I hurried inside as the biting cold felt like it was damn near chasing me.

Paula was in the kitchen bagging mollies, weed, and heroine.

"Hey, Paula. How you doin'?"

"What's up, Simone? What are you doing here?"

"Grabbing some of Omari's things. I won't be long."

"Yea, you betta get outta here. Your bougie ass

don't belong in no trap, baby."

We both giggled as I headed down the hall. I bypassed what was Omari's old bedroom and slipped into the pantry. I took my heels off in order to be as quiet as possible and disappeared into the back of the pantry. In the furthest corner was a lose floorboard that I opened. In the floor was Omari's drug stash. I took three bricks from the stash and put them in my Celine tote. Then, while on my knees, I crawled to the front of the pantry to make sure that Paula was still posted at the kitchen table. She was, so I crept out of the pantry and headed into the bedroom to grab what of Omari's things that were still there.

FOURTEEN

OMARI

"What's up, Capone?"

"We got a problem, boss."

I wasn't in the mood to hear no shit like that. It was too early in the morning for dumb shit.

"What's the problem?"

"We have a thief in the crib."

"A thief? Which crib? What's missing?"

"Three bricks are missing from the spot in Riverdale."

My stomach did three summersaults so serious that I got a little sick. Three bricks was worth at least ninety-thousand dollars on the street.

"Somebody broke in?"

As Capone replied, "Hell naw," I went ahead and got out of the bed. It was obvious that I was gone have to hit the block much earlier than usual. "When Chance told me that the count was off, first thing I assumed was Ching. But them niggas wouldn't come in here for three bricks."

"Hell naw they wouldn't."

"You think Chance grabbed them?"

"Hell naw, man. You don't come off to me as that type of dude."

"Paula?"

"She swears to God it wasn't her."

I moaned and groaned in frustration as I climbed out of bed. This shit wasn't cool. It put me in a fucked up position because whoever stole the shit had to get dealt with. The only nigga I was focused on dealing with at the moment was Ching, who was still somewhere hiding. He hadn't been to any of his spots. Black, Smoke, and Burt ran most of his errands. Ching had disappeared.

Ching wasn't a punk. He wasn't a runner. He wasn't the type of nigga to just let me get away with shooting at him and stealing from him. I knew at some point he would resurface. I had to find him before he found me.

"You at the spot?"

"Hell yea."

"Be there in a minute."

I hung up, threw the cell on the bed, and just paced with my head in my hands. I did not want to deal with this shit. Everybody that worked for me, I fucked with heavy. I trusted every block boy and every hype with my life. They were loyal.

But they knew me not to be some crazy trigger happy savage. So it was possible that one of them was taking my kindness for weakness.

"What's wrong, babe?"

Simone came into the room wearing a black long sleeve sweater maxi dress that fell to her ankles and over a pair of Christian Louboutin boots that cost me three thousand dollars. Her pudgy stomach stuck out of the cashmere.

She really wasn't on my good side either. She went to the doctor without me again, and it really pissed me the fuck off. She was treating me like I was some nigga too busy to be a part of my child's life, when she knew that I would go over and beyond to do every and anything for my children.

She watched me pace curiously.

"Somebody stole some work out the spot," I told her, answering her curiosity.

Her eyes bucked as she took her usual seat at the vanity. Her hair was already done. Now she was doing her makeup.

"Who do think did it and when?"

"Ain't no tellin'. We only go in the stash when we gotta make more packs."

"Your people wouldn't steal from you."

"I didn't think so, but apparently somebody did."

"Maybe it was Tiana."

Though they had ruled out abuse and stopped investigating Tiana and her boyfriend, I still hadn't been fucking with her. I heard from her brother, Fred, that she felt some type of way about that. But he was so loyal to me that he was also mad at Tiana for having that dude in my crib anyway.

I pondered over the thought as Simone continued to convince me. "She still has a key."

"It would honestly make me feel better if she was the one that did it. At least it wouldn't be one of my people turning on me."

CHANCE

I felt weird as hell looking at Lexington House. I hadn't seen it since I left for transitional housing last year. It's funny how sitting in that parking lot felt like being at home.

Back then, I hated being there. I hated my life. I was lost.

At that moment, I would have given anything to go back to that place in life. Now I was realizing that my past was a cakewalk compared to the shit that I was facing now.

Ever since leaving Lexington, I had hit roadblock after roadblock.

The biggest boldest dirtiest roadblock in my life came walking towards my car in a black sweater dress. I noticed that she was either pregnant or had gained some weight.

When she opened the door and sat in my car, the smell of Aqua Di Gioia overpowered the smell of weed that Capone left in there earlier that day.

"Here," was all that she said as she handed me a plastic bag. It was heavy. I looked in it curiously and immediately recognized the bricks.

"Tuh," I grunted. This chick was unbelievable. "So

you the one who stole them bricks."

"Yes, for you. That's worth almost a hundred thousand dollars. Now you can leave."

I wasn't excited. Had she bought these bricks with her own money, this would be great. If I took these three bricks and left town, I would never be able to come back to Chicago due to the price on my head that Omari and Capone would put there because they would assume that my disappearance was due to me stealing from them. I couldn't just go to Minnesota either. I would have to go so far that word of my come up and whereabouts didn't make it back to the Chi.

"Was Omari at the spot when you left?"

I shook my head, barely paying attention to what she was saying because my thoughts were taking over.

"Where is he? Do you know?"

"He and Capone moved all the product out of the spot on Riverdale. They takin' it out south."

I sighed heavily as the bricks lay on my lap.

Simone saw me contemplating. "Chance, this isn't money, but this is your opportunity to leave and start all over. You can work for yourself. You don't have to stand on some block all winter anymore."

I didn't want to leave. I liked my life. I had done

some pretty terrible things, but I finally liked my life. I liked my homies. The thought of just walking away from Gia tugged at my heart, but knowing that I was also walking away from that pussy damn near brought a tear to my eye.

Noticing my reluctance, Simone began to beg me to leave. "Please, Chance."

She slipped her hand softly on my thigh. I immediately smacked her arm so hard that her hand flew off and she screeched out in my pain.

"Nigga…"

She called herself getting hype, but my anger far surpassed hers. I was damn near in the passenger seat with her as my rage poured out of me like smoke as I pointed aggressively at her face.

"You lyin' ass, bitch! You can stop playing these fucking mind games! Don't fucking touch me!"

Simone just sat there, coolly and innocent, as always.

Finally, my anger subsided. Reluctantly, I put the bricks in the backseat on the floor. The happiness in Simone couldn't be hidden, no matter how hard she tried to act nonchalantly at my conceding to yet another one of her devious moves.

"Get the fuck out of my car, Simone."

"Are you leaving?"

"GET THE FUCK OUT!"

The audacity of this bitch sent my anger off the meter. I reached over her, opened the door, and started pushing her so hard that she had to get out of the car before she fell out. It took everything in me not to beat the shit out of her like I wanted to. She had taken everything from me and still was. I was still a pawn in her game just to get another man.

I was mad at her for being a conniving bitch, but I was angrier with myself for being so weak.

I was putting the car in reverse before she was even able to slam the car door. Then I sped off and out of the parking lot. I never wanted to see that bitch again.

SIMONE

I let out a big sigh of relief as I watched Chance speed out of the parking lot. I didn't give a fuck how mad he got, he needed to leave town. Though he didn't tell me that he was leaving or when, I knew that he was. He was young, but he was far from stupid.

Now that Chance was out of the way, I had one more trick up my sleeve before I headed home. I noticed how much better I felt as I drove towards the suburbs. Getting Chance out of Chicago had been such a burden. However, the burden was lifting rapidly by the second.

When I pulled up in front of the house in Riverdale, I spotted Fred on post.

I rolled my window down and asked, "Is Paula in there?"

"Yea, Simone. She in there. What's up?"

"Tell her to come here."

Then I hurriedly rolled my window back up to block out the cold. It was almost April, but it was still barely the high forties during the day. It always took Chicago a long time to convert from winter to spring.

About a minute passed before Paula came bouncing out of the house. Her hair had grown longer, but it was unkempt. It was dirty blond hair that fell almost to her butt, but it was literally dirty and appeared to be greasy. She was an older hype. Paula had to be in her forties. Because of the drugs, she looked to be in her late fifties. Skin that was once clear and pink was now filthy with needle marks, bruises, and deterioration from the drugs. Her body was frail and looked weak and sickly.

When she got in my car, I could smell the funk all over her. She probably hadn't showered in days. I rolled down the window with my nose turned up.

"Hey, Simone."

She shivered from the cold. She didn't even have on a coat. She had on the same worn and dirty Abercrombie hoodie that she'd worn all winter.

"I have a job for you. You aren't going anywhere anytime soon, are you?"

I was the one that put Omari up on Paula. I often times saw her begging downtown around my condo. One time, I even saw her going through the trash. I knew that she was on drugs, so when Omari needed the trap out south cleaned, or any other odd job, I told him about Paula. Then she eventually started cooking and cutting heroin for him, amongst other things.

The pay was lucrative for her, but hypes did shit like disappear without notice. They fell off the map here and there, ran away, or got themselves clean out of nowhere.

"I don't plan on it," she said with a laugh. "What kind of job?"

"I need you to help me steal a baby."

Paula laughed initially, but when she saw that I hadn't cracked a smile, she took me seriously.

"What the fuck?"

"You heard me."

When Omari told me that his sister was having a c-section, that's when it dawned on me. I could take Erica's baby. They were siblings, so, hopefully, the baby would look similar to Omari; hopefully even having those genetically strong gray eyes.

I had it all planned out, so I shared with Paula the plan that I had been weaving together for weeks. Since Erica was scheduled to have her c-section in a few weeks when she was seven months, I would tell Omari that I was scheduled out of town for a speaking engagement with my job far away in Texas somewhere, too far for Omari to get to in time when I called him frantically saying that I was going into premature labor. Instead, I would be in

Indianapolis, waiting on Erica to leave the hospital with her baby. Then Paula would car jack her, taking the baby with her.

Given the distance in Erica and Blood's relationship, I assumed that I could pull this off. I didn't even know if Erica knew that I was supposedly pregnant. The way that things were playing out, she and Omari would never see each other again, so I could get away with this if I played it ever so carefully.

I know I sounded insane and irrational. Even Paula looked at me like I was a lunatic. I kinda had gone insane. Trying to come up with a way to get myself out of this impractical ass pregnancy lie that I had spun was driving me absolutely crazy. But the more Omari lovingly touched my belly and called me the mother of his child, I could not bear to take another child from him by lying and saying that I lost this baby because I would not be able to realistically produce one.

"You are crazy as hell, Simone," Paula replied shaking her head and nervously looking out of the window.

I grabbed her arm and snatched her towards me, making her give me her full attention. My eyes looked beady, scary, and obsessed. I knew it, because Paula was cringing in fear.

I needed Paula's help because I definitely couldn't pull this off on my own. Erica would spot me for sure. But she would never know who Paula was. I wasn't scared of Paula telling. She loved that dope too much to risk losing her spot in Omari's kitchen.

Holding her arm in my hand and digging my acrylic nails into her weakening skin, I threatened her. "Crazy or not, you will help me, or I will tell Omari that I saw you stealing those three bricks."

Paula gasped. "No, I didn't!"

"As far as I know, you did."

I aggressively released her arm and she rubbed it in agony. "Okay. All right. I'll help you."

GIA

Chance and I were at the White Palace having breakfast. It was two in the morning. I had just left Sunset, along with Chance who'd spent his evening kicking it there. Chance was at Sunset so much that the bouncers and bartenders knew him well, so being there was like hanging with friends at this point, not just going to see some ass and titties.

Things had gotten better between me and Chance since my outburst a few days ago when he couldn't keep an erection. I guess he peeped how he was acting and redirected his anger. He was back to his normal, attentive, and caring self.

Things were finally getting back to normal.

So I thought and so I was feeling, until Chance dropped a bomb on me.

Sitting across from me playing in his omelet, he told me, "I need to leave town for a minute."

"Excuse me?"

He hadn't said that he was taking a trip or making a run for Omari. This sounded permanent, so I instantly got an attitude.

"I said that I need to leave…"

"I heard you! Why?"

He ran his hand over his head and continued to play in his food without answering me.

"Chance."

I couldn't believe that he was acting like this. I figured that whatever it was that had been bothering him, whatever it was that was making him run, didn't have anything to do with me. We weren't in love, but I hoped that the time we spent together would at least deserve some sensitivity and respect.

"Chance, answer me."

"I can't." He finally looked me in my eyes. I noticed how weary and tired they were. He was back to being the sad and lonely boy that I met at the strip club a few months ago.

"You can't?" But I didn't care how weary or tired he was. I had given him what I hadn't been willing to give any man in years; me. He convinced me to put my wall down, to let him in, to trust him, and now he was too much of a pussy to handle whatever business he needed to, rather than walking away and just fucking leaving me here to wallow in grief.

"When are you leaving?"

"My flight leaves in a couple of hours."

My eyes fell out of my sockets. "A couple of hours?! How long have you known that you were leaving?"

"Not that long. I just got the ticket yesterday." He noticed my tears and sighed. "Are you crying?"

"Hell yes, I'm crying. You've been laying up in my crib and fucking me, but didn't even have the decency to tell me that you were leaving."

"We're not even in a relationship, Gia."

"And?!"

"I didn't mean it like that. I meant, I didn't think you would care this much. I didn't think it would hurt you."

I was livid. Literally, my heart was beating so fast with anger and shock that I was becoming short of breath. "You didn't think it would hurt me? Are you serious?"

"Then come with me, Gia."

I looked at him like he was crazy. "I can't come with you! I can't just up and leave. Like you just said, we aren't even in a relationship."

"Then why are you crying?"

"Fuck you," left my lips before I knew it.

He wasn't worth the explanation. He wasn't worth my tears. Come to find out, he wasn't even worth me letting my guard down, and he definitely wasn't worth Rae.

I stood from the table and walked away. I kinda wanted him to follow me. I kinda wanted him to profess his love for me, despite me knowing that there was no real love between us. I just needed to hear something that justified how I had stupidly let a piece of dick sway me into the same trap of a disloyal lying ass nigga.

FIFTEEN

OMARI

It was almost four in the morning. I was riding down the e-way towards Simone's crib. My cell phone rang. It was a number that I didn't recognize. Nor was it saved in my contacts.

"Hello?"

"Whad up, nephew?"

I almost veered off of the road. I fought to keep control of my Challenger, to keep it from swaying over to the shoulder of the expressway.

I had been looking for this nigga for weeks. But just like I assumed, he wasn't going to let me get away with this shit for long.

Before I could say anything, he told me, "Come holla at me."

Though he was coming at me like a man, I figured that this might be a set up. Yet, I still salivated at the thought of putting him in the same ground that he put Aeysha in, so I complied without a second thought.

"Where you at?"

He was parked in front this abandoned building on 63rd and Carpenter. At four in the morning and with it being barely twenty degrees outside, the streets were completely dark and completely quiet. As I crawled down the block, I saw Ching's Range Rover running just where he said it would be. Smoke spilled out of the exhaust as I pulled up behind it. Something told me that I should shoot Capone a text message, but I decided against it. This was between me and Ching. There was no need to keep making other people a part of it.

I still watched my back though. I grabbed my pistol from underneath my seat and held it tightly with my finger on the trigger. The metal was cold against my skin. I looked through the windows of the Range Rover and saw that Ching was the only one inside.

I could hear the locks popping just as I reached the passenger side of the vehicle. I opened the door cautiously; expecting for gunfire to meet me. Yet, Ching was simply sitting in the seat rolling a blunt. I could hear Jay Z's voice faintly.

Once I slipped into the passenger seat, he noticed the gun that I was holding, he noticed how my finger was still on the trigger, and he chuckled. "Are you serious, man?"

"I told you months ago that I had a bullet waiting on yo' ass on this side if you ever got out."

My nerve and bravery took him by surprise. "You know, I was hoping that you were just going through some fucked up shit because of what happened to Aeysha. Your mother told my mother that you been pretty fucked up behind her murder. That's why I let you get away with this bullshit you been pullin'…"

"You ain't let me get away with shit. You shot up my spot."

"No, my block boys shot up your spot. You shot one of them. You think they was gone let you get away with that shit?"

"Just like I ain't lettin' you get away with killing Aeysha."

"I didn't kill Aeysha."

"Yes, you did."

"Nephew…"

"Stop calling me that shit!" I aimed the gun at his head before I knew it. The barrel of my pistol hit his temple so hard that it slightly knocked his head into the window.

To my surprise, he didn't react. He didn't move. He didn't retaliate. He just sat in the driver's seat, motionless, while I held the pistol against his dome.

"I'm not your fucking nephew, motherfucka! I'm not your family! Family don't do what the fuck you did! You killed her!"

He had the balls to turn towards me. The gun was pointing right between his eyes.

"If I was bogus enough to kill her, don't you think that you would be dead by now? You've stolen over a quarter million dollars worth of dope from me. You've made me look like a punk ass nigga to my entire camp because I ain't popped yo' ass."

I didn't try to stop my tears from falling. It hurt me to the point of great sadness that I was about to blow the brains out of a man that I looked up to for all of my life, a man that ended up hurting me in a way that I will never get over.

At the same time, it brought such tears of joy to me that I was finally about to show Aeysha that I was the man that I always wanted to be for her, protecting her with all of my ability.

SIMONE

When I woke up that morning, it caught me off guard that Omari wasn't there. He sent me a text message during the middle of the night saying that he was still at the spot but would be home shortly. I was so sleepy that I didn't even respond.

Before going to shower for work, I called him a few times, but didn't get an answer. I figured that he'd gotten too drunk to drive and decided to spend the night at one of the spots. That had happened a few times in the past. I was actually appreciative that he wasn't home. I didn't have to force myself to regurgitate like I usually did while in the bathroom in the morning.

I hated throwing up. I hated those fucking prenatal pills. And I definitely hated how fat I was letting myself get.

Yet, it would all be over soon. As I dressed for work, I imagined how beautiful Erica's baby would be. I gloated in the thought of Omari and me bathing our baby boy for the first time. I relished in the joy of our family finally being complete. In the same instance, I would be destroying the happily ever after that Tre played me for. The idea made me incredibly happy.

I called Omari's phone a few more times as I gathered my purse and handbag. Again, I didn't get an answer. I sent him a text message asking him to call me as soon as he woke up to let me know that he was okay. I thought that maybe I should drive by the spots just to make sure that he was there. My natural female insecurities began to surface. When I met Omari, he had a woman for years and yet fucked me relentlessly with no problem. I got sick with worry, wondering if he had gone back to his old ways and that I was starting to reap what I sowed.

I was so wrapped up in my thoughts as I left out of the condo that I had no idea that someone was standing on the other side of the front door until he was so close that his large stature overshadowed me. At first I was relieved, assuming that the man was Omari. But when I recognized who it really was, my relief turned into panic.

When our eyes met, my heart fell to the deepest pit of my stomach and I became weak with pure terror. Chills that felt like death feverishly ran down my spine. As he charged towards me, I was suddenly extremely sorrowful for everything that I had done. For the first time, I was sorry for killing Aeysha. I was especially remorseful for smothering that poor baby to death. I condemned myself over and over again.

I attempted to fight back as he grabbed me around my neck, but he was so powerful as he attacked me that I could feel my acrylic nails ripping away from my fingertips as my hands collided with his attack.

I clawed at his hand around my neck while trying desperately to breathe, hoping that someone would come out of their home and see our confrontation.

"No! Stop!" I tried to scream, but his hand was so tight around my throat that I could barely get out the words. "Jimmy, no!"

CHANCE

I was leaving that morning. By the time Capone and Omari
woke up and did their rounds at the spots, I would be on a
flight to Georgia.

"I just came to get my things."

Gia stood in her doorway with annoyance all over
her face. I hadn't seen her since she walked out on me
earlier that morning at the restaurant. I hadn't followed her
once she stormed out. I simply sat at the table in White
Palace trying to figure out a way to get around leaving
Chicago. I didn't want to leave, and seeing Gia's reaction
made me want to stay even more.

But even though I wracked my brain, it was evident
that I didn't have a choice but to get on the flight. So, about
thirty minutes ago, I finally left the restaurant.

Proof of Gia's pain was all over her face. Her
makeup was smeared. Her hair was all over her head. I
knew that she hadn't been to sleep.

She reluctantly moved out of the way to let me in. I
promised myself to make this quick. I only had a few things
in her room that I needed to grab; clothes, shoes, hats, and a
stash of cash in her drawer.

I wanted to make it quick because I knew that I was hurting her. I knew that my distance and dry attitude towards leaving was making her regret every moment she had spent with me. But there was no way that I could explain this shit to her. It was for her own good that I just bounced without telling her anything.

I didn't want to leave her. I would have given anything to stay in the Chi, fucking her and working alongside Omari and Capone, but that shit was too risky. It was time for me to bounce. I convinced myself that I could create a similar life in Georgia.

"Gia…"

I wanted to apologize. She sat on the couch with tears in her eyes. I knew that leaving wasn't what was pissing her off. It was the fact that on top of Rae killing herself damn near in front of her, I was pulling this move. She was pissed at my nerve. She was pissed at me for not living up to my bargain of being real.

I couldn't blame her.

She cut off my apology by cutting her eyes at me. I sighed heavily, deciding not to say anything and just bounce. I rested my keys and phone on the coffee table and disappeared into her bedroom a few feet away.

I felt like shit for so many reasons. Gia and I had

talked about her trust issues with men for hours. When we first met, she told me so many stories of niggas fucking her over to the point that she was open to Rae's affectionate, loving, and trusting lesbian relationship.

I hated to be another man on her list that hurt her. I wasn't in love with her, but I cared for her and was looking forward to the day that we made the commitment to be together forever. I wanted her to know that I was leaving against my own will and that I would do anything to change the things that I'd done in my past that made it impossible for me to stay in Chicago.

Leaving was something that I had to do. She wouldn't understand but, by the way my life was going, I figured she was better off without me anyway.

"Who the fuck is Simone?!"

Gia's shouts caught me off guard as I was throwing my clothes into a duffle bag. I spun around, looking at her like she was crazy. That's when my keys, which were once flying through the air, smacked me dead in the nose.

"'Why did you do this to me?' 'You were supposed to be with me'!"

I held my face as I picked up my keys from the floor. All the while, the words that Gia was quoting sounded so eerily familiar. I recognized them as text messages that I had been sending to Simone in frustration. My heart sank, realizing what Gia thought she'd read.

"You lying son of a bitch!"

Then she threw my phone across the room. I was able to catch it before it hit me in the face as well.

Gia continuously screamed as tears streamed down her face. "Get the fuck out!! NOW! GET THE FUCK OUT!!"

OMARI

I was flying down the expressway when Capone finally called me back.

I hurriedly turned down Chief Keef and answered the phone with, "Meet me at my crib."

"What? Nigga, its seven o'clock in the morning."

"You don't sound sleep."

Capone laughed slyly. "Naw, I wasn't."

Then I heard some little cute girlish giggle so close that it sounded like she was on three way with us.

"Get out the pussy and meet me at the condo. It's been a hell of a morning."

"Word?"

"Word."

"See you in a minute."

"One."

Since Capone had got a spot not too far from Simone's, I knew that he would be there within minutes, just as I was.

As soon as I hung up, I called Simone's cell again. Again, I didn't get an answer. She left for work at seven o'clock every day, so I knew that she wasn't sleep. I was sure that she was probably pissed that I was out all night and hadn't been answering her calls.

I knew she thought that I was in some pussy all night.

I blew her phone up all the way to the crib, all while trying to wrap my head around how things went down with Ching.

Capone was pulling up in front of my crib at the same time I was.

As soon as he got out of the car, he was barking at me with eyes that were riding low and hazy. "Man, what the fuck is going on?"

"I got some shit to tell you. C'mon, let's go in the crib."

I was busy dialing Simone's cell again as Capone asked me over and over again what the fuck was going on. But now I was more so worried about Simone then telling him about what went down earlier that morning. Simone had never gotten upset with me so much that she ignored my calls. With her being pregnant, I was especially worried.

Still, Capone was all over me, wondering what the emergency was. As I unlocked the door, he nagged me over and over again. I'm sure he noticed how wired I was and how whatever happened had me freaking out. "Man, what the fuck is…"

As I opened the door, Capone stopped dead in his tracks.

"Oh shit," slipped from my mouth as my eyes fell on Simone lying on the kitchen floor, unconscious.

"Fuck!" Full of panic and dread, I ran towards her as fast I could. "Call 9-1-1!"

GIA

I was so mad! Even though Chance had left out of my home with his tail between his legs, it wasn't enough. I drove at record speeds in pure shock at what I'd read in his phone.

I felt like I was being Catfished. I just knew that at any moment, Ashton Kutcher was going to jump out from behind a tree with a camera crew and tell me that I was being punk'd.

The level of Chance's deceit sickened me literally. I saw myself trusting him, cooking for him, sucking his dick, and fucking him, and fought the urge to scream in anger as I drove down 79th Street. These niggas talk you into putting your guard down with no intent but to shit on you and fuck up your life with no mercy.

I took care of that son of a bitch. I gave him somewhere to lay his head when all he had was that filthy ass motel to sleep in. I cooked him meals when he didn't even have a fucking dollar to buy a double cheeseburger off the dollar menu at McDonald's.

Rae killed herself. Rae was dead all because I was too far up in this lying niggas ass to make sure that she was okay.

All of that for this; a nigga who was completely opposite of what he showed me. He whoo'd me while lying to me. He manipulated the fuck outta me while holding me and calling me his wife.

I wasn't going to let him get away with it. He was the first nigga to fuck me over in a long time, but I was going to be the first bitch that fucked him over.

I parked sloppily, hopped out of the car, and literally ran towards the door. People looked at me like I was crazy. They saw my tears. They saw my hair sticking up every which way all over my head. They saw the distress in my eyes and watched me curiously; wondering what my problem was.

My problem was that I had stupidly trusted again. I had been laying up with a man that I had just found out was not only a liar but a monster.

"Yes, ma'am? Can I help you?" The officer at the front desk gave me the same peculiar stares that everyone had in the precinct parking lot. But I wasn't trying to hide my distress. I didn't give a fuck. Chance was going to pay for fucking me over.

"I need to speak to a homicide detective," I said nearly out of breath with a voice cracking with anxiety and hurt. "I have information about a murder."

To be continued . . .

Please be sure to leave your review of this novel!
Jessica would love to hear your thoughts!

Follow Jessica online:
Twitter: @authorjwatkins
Instagram: @authorjwatkins
Facebook: www.facebook.com/authorjwatkins
Facebook Fan Club:
www.facebook.com/groups/femistryfans